I AM NOT ESTHER

I AM NOT ESTHER

FLEUR BEALE

HYPERION PAPERBACKS
NEW YORK

Text copyright © 1998 by Fleur Beale
First published by Longacre Press in 1998

For information address Hyperion Books for Children,
114 Fifth Avenue, New York, New York 10011-5690.
Printed in the United States of America
First Hyperion Paperback edition, 2004
1 3 5 7 9 10 8 6 4 2

Cover photo © 2002 by Roxann Arwen Mills/Photonica
Designed by Gail Doobinin
This book is set in 11-point Meridien.
Library of Congress Cataloging-in-Publication Data
Beale, Fleur.
I am not Esther/ Fleur Beale.— 1st. American ed.
p.   cm.
Summary: After her mother unexpectedly leaves her with her
uncle's family—members of a fanatical Christian cult—Kirby tries
to learn what has become of her mother and struggles to cope with
the repressiveness of her new surroundings and to maintain
her own identity.
ISBN 0-7868-1673-2
[1. Cults—Fiction. 2. Identity—Fiction. 3. Mothers and daughters—
Fiction. 4. Christian life—Fiction.] I. Title.
PZ7.B35684 Iae 2002
[Fic]—dc21
2002027256

Visit www.hyperionteens.com

TO TIM 1946–1998,
AND TO OUR DAUGHTERS
BRIDGET AND PENNY

1

I CAME HOME FROM SCHOOL on the last day of term, and my mother was crying. I rushed to her, threw my arms around her. "What's wrong? What's the matter?" I hugged her hard and hoped the world wasn't ending. She *never* cried. Never.

She choked, sniffed, and sat up straight. "Sorry, Kirby. I'm fine. Really. Just ghosts from the past. Put it down to Christmas. Don't they say Christmas brings out all sorts of stresses?" She managed an almost normal smile. "How about we have tea in town? There's a new restaurant David told me about. Yummy food, he says."

"Is David hassling you?"

Her hands twitched and her body jerked like a marionette. "Of course not! No guy hassles me. You know that!"

I didn't, but the problem probably wasn't David. He was a nurse at the same hospital as Mum and he was a riot, but definitely not the type to want to get into a relationship with. So we went out for tea, and Mum was bright and funny as she always is. "What ghosts?" I asked, digging into my "Disgustingly Sinful Chocolate Pudding."

Mum shook her head. "Just things. Ignore them, and they'll go away."

"They don't seem to have," I remarked. "Aren't you supposed to get things out in the open? Confront them, and then they go away?" I'd read that in a magazine the day before.

Mum shook her head. "Nah. Starve them to death, I say. Keep them in the dark."

"Drown them with tears." The words were out before I had thought what I was saying, but Mum just pulled a face.

"They should be well dead, then."

"But you never cry," I said.

"Not since you took over the budget," she said,

and giggled. "I'm so hopeless with money! Why am I so hopeless, Kirby?"

I could have said, *Because you're a sucker for a sob story*, or, *Because you help Louisa and her kids so much*, or, *Because you're a dizzy flake who shops till she drops*. But what I did say was, "I dunno."

Whatever the ghosts were, my mother had them well shut back in their box and she wasn't going to talk about them. The same way she'd never talk when I tried to get her to tell me about when she was a kid and her family and everything. She'd shudder and throw her hands in the air. "Don't ask, Kirby! They were ghastly, and I got out of there on my sixteenth birthday." Then she'd look at me and grin. "One day I might tell you the whole horrible story." And we'd both chorus, "But I doubt it!" and collapse in a heap of giggles.

She was fun, my dizzy flake of a mother. I loved her passionately, and I didn't care that I was the one who had to organize the running of our flat, who had to write out the checks for the bills, make sure she didn't spend all the money before the next payday, get the washing done, drag her off to buy groceries. "Shopping's so boring, Kirby!" she'd cry.

"So's being hungry," I said every week.

Neither did I miss having relatives. There was only Mum and me, but our neighbors in the next flat—Louisa and her three kids—were like family. Gemma, the oldest, was my best friend. It was Louisa who'd taught me how to budget and how to shop for groceries and all the stuff Mum wasn't interested in.

Sometimes I couldn't quite believe that Mum was such a good nurse, but she was. Patients often gave her stuff when they left, and some came round and visited. "She made me laugh," one old lady said. "I'm sure I got better because I laughed so much."

"She was so efficient," a man with gray hair and one eye said, "but so alive! Better than a painkiller, more fun than a bottle of whiskey. She really loves people, that lady."

The thing that stuck in my mind from that little lot was the word *efficient*. My mother—efficient?

The tears on the last day of school were the first clue I had that something might be wrong. I put all the other crazy stuff down to Christmas, and there was a heap more than usual of it. Mum took Louisa and the two boys shopping and they all came home loaded with parcels and giggling. She pushed money at me and Gemma and told us to have ourselves a ball. I knew darned well there wasn't going to be enough money to stretch through until next payday, but what could I say? There was Gemma practically crying because she'd never had so much money all to herself before. So we hit town, and she bought jean shorts and a skimpy top that Louisa was going to throw a fit about, and I tried on a million things and bought nothing.

Then when we got home we found that Mum had decided to have a barbecue, so that day ended with twenty of the neighbors in our back garden even though Mum had to go on duty at eleven.

The next day she had two hours sleep and got up and cleaned the flat from floor to ceiling.

"Give it a rest!" I yelled. Gemma and I were watching *Endless Summer II*, for the ninth time, it's true, but still, a girl likes to concentrate.

There were two weeks between when school broke up and Christmas. Mum was worse than dizzy, she was frenetic. She dragged me and Gemma all over Auckland looking for just the right Christmas decorations. She went to parties, she worked, she stole the plastic money card when I wasn't looking and hung around in town giving money to people who looked desperate.

"She's driving me nuts!" I yelled, slamming Louisa's door.

"Something's going on," Louisa said. "Must be something to do with those creepy guys who've been visiting."

"What guys? I don't know anything about creepy guys visiting!" I stared at Louisa.

"You don't?" Her eyebrows disappeared under her gray hair, and she gave the Christmas cake she was making an extra-hard belting. "They've been coming for months on and off. Always when you're at school. I asked her about them, but she just laughed and said it wasn't anything she couldn't handle."

I sat down on a stool, feeling decidedly shaky. Mum always told me everything, except about when she was a kid. Why hadn't she told me about this?

"Because it's my business and nobody else's," she said when I asked her. She glared at me, and I could almost hear her hair crackling with determination. Her lips were jammed together in a tight line, and her eyes fairly blazed.

I didn't know what to do, and Louisa obviously didn't either. So I did what we always did, Mum and me—shrugged my shoulders and hoped that it, or they, would go away. Mum laughed and tweaked my hair. "Let's dye our hair for Christmas! Green and red and silver!"

So we did. Louisa laughed till she cried, but Gemma said, "You wanna look like a disaster? You look like a disaster!"

I didn't care. Mum was happy, I was happy, it was Christmas. Why worry?

The tinsel fell off the tree on Christmas Eve. Mum got a pile of mail. I sorted it out from the sixteen bits of junk mail and gave it to her. "Some people aren't very well organized," I said. "Of course, you sent all your cards a month ago."

"Of course," she said. She always sent out what she called New Year cards, because she reckoned there wasn't enough time to do cards before Christmas. She tore the first couple open and tossed them on to me. One was from a patient, the other from her mate David at the hospital. On the front of the card was a particularly spaced-out-looking angel, and he'd written, *This reminded me of you, dear Ellen. Can't think why! Love to you and the poisonous brat, party heaps XX David.*

I was still chuckling when I happened to look up and see that my mother had gone perfectly white.

There wasn't a scrap of color in her face, and a strand of silver hair lay starkly across her cheek. She was holding a single piece of paper in her hand, but she was staring blankly somewhere beyond it. I was terrified. "Mum! Mum! Stop it!" I jumped up and shook her. "What's the matter? Tell me!" I tried to take the letter, but she snatched it and scrunched it into the pocket of her shorts.

"I'm okay. I'm fine. Just a bit of a shock. Not to worry, it'll be all right. Get me a drink of water, will you, Kirby?" She sat down, shaking a bit, but she seemed to have a wall around her that wouldn't let me in.

I filled a glass and passed it to her.

"Thanks." She didn't drink it. Just held it in her hands, then she put it carefully on the table. "Well. That's it then." She took a couple of deep breaths and fixed her big eyes on my face.

"What?" I asked, feeling as if I was walking in a mixture of mud and fog. "What d'you mean—*that's it*? What's in that letter? Something's wrong!"

"Calm down!" She patted the chair beside her and her hand shook. She quickly put it in her lap and held it with her other one. "Sit." She nodded at the chair. Then she told me very quietly and calmly that she'd just been accepted to work on a refugee program, and that we'd be moving to Wellington the day after Boxing Day.

Words can hit you in the gut. These left me winded and breathless and sick. "You can't do this," I croaked. "You're not serious!"

Her arms crept up to hug themselves around her body as if she was holding herself together. "I've never been more serious in my life, Kirby. And I have to get away. Do something different." She stared at me with eyes that didn't quite meet mine. "I've been so stressed lately."

I managed to force some words out. "But it's all so sudden."

She put a hand that felt cold and clammy over mine. "I know, my darling. And I'm sorry."

She stood up and picked up the car keys.

"Where are you going?" I shrieked.

She spoke in a quiet voice that terrified me. "I have to go and fix it up with work."

With that, she disappeared out the door, still wearing her old shorts and the T-shirt streaked with hair dye.

I tottered over to Louisa's and collapsed in a heap on her couch. Gemma cried with me. Louisa tried to talk to Mum when she got home, but Mum wouldn't listen, wouldn't stay still. She packed up the flat, put the big stuff in storage, but gave away about half our possessions.

"You can't do that!" I yelled, grabbing back my old stuffed elephant.

"All right!" she yelled back. "You do it, then!"

"Do it yourself! You're the one that wants to go! You go by yourself," I screamed. "I'll stay here with Louisa!"

But Louisa couldn't afford another kid, and Mum would get lost driving to Wellington. She'd probably end up in Gisborne. Serve her right if she did.

It was a horrible Christmas. Mum didn't even try to make it fun. She kept on packing things up and wiping down surfaces that were already shiningly clean. When she sat down, her hands twitched.

"What's the matter? Tell me!" I kept begging, but she'd just shake her head and fold her lips together and get busy doing something else.

We packed our old heap of a car on the evening of Boxing Day, and we drove out of Auckland and our old lives forever early the next morning. I told Louisa and Gemma not to get up to see us off because I'd only cry. Louisa hugged me. "You know

I'm always here, no matter what."

I sniffed. I did know it, but here was going to be a long way from where we were going to be.

Mum seemed to relax a bit as she drove. She still wouldn't talk to me about anything except to say, "I've always wanted to work with refugees, Kirby. I had to grab the chance when it came."

"It's dumb and it doesn't make sense," I burst out. "If you're stressed now, you're going to be a heap worse coping with a new job."

She shook her head. "Different people. New challenges. No time to think of myself. It's what I need."

"But how come they let you leave the hospital so quickly? I thought you had to give notice and all that stuff."

"They owed me some holidays," she said.

But we'd taken holidays in September and gone to Hanmer Springs so we could lie around in hot pools and look at mountains at the same time. I glanced at her. She might be acting a bit calmer now, but she was still jumpy. "Mum . . ." I said tentatively.

"Leave it, Kirby. Just leave it!" So we said nothing until we got to Hamilton, when I said I was hungry.

I ate a couple of hamburgers, but she only had a cup of tea. As we traveled down the island, the only times she spoke were to ask me for directions. I held the map on my lap and wished I had a map of her mind as well.

In the middle of the afternoon when the tar on the road was melting with the heat, the old heap sighed and stopped.

Mum sat there, grasping the wheel so tightly her knuckles turned ivory.

"Mum," I spoke calmly. "It's okay. We're in a town. We're lucky." I looked around for a name. "Foxton. We're in Foxton." I suddenly felt better. This was what I was used to doing. Looking after my mother. Picking up the bits when things went wrong. Organizing her. "We are going over to that coffee bar and we are going to have something to eat and drink. Then we'll find someone to look at the heap." Which actually meant I would find the someone.

I got out and yanked on her door to get it open. She stumbled out. I took her arm and steered her across the road, holding her back from walking under a truck.

I dragged her up a couple of steps, then shoved her toward a table and chairs. Sat her down, bought her coffee and sandwiches. "Look," I said, "we don't have to go on with this. How about I phone Louisa? She'd come down and get us."

Mum just shook her head. "It's something I have to do. You don't understand." She was right. I didn't. I stood and stared down at her bent head. She wasn't going to talk, so I'd never understand. I shrugged. Might as well get on with it.

The mechanic I found didn't understand why a fourteen-year-old girl would be trying to get a car fixed, but he did it. "It might get you to Wellington," he said in the sort of voice people use when they say you might win Lotto.

I retrieved Mum. "He says it'll get us there." I should have lied and told her it had died, but in the mood she was in, she'd have made us hitchhike— and that I could do without.

The car held together long enough, and we stopped for the night at a motel somewhere a bit north of the city. Mum walked around and around the lounge, twitching at bedcovers, kicking chairs, picking up cushions and beating them up.

I went out and bought some fish-and-chips. I ate them; she didn't touch them. She loves fish-and-chips. She'd live on them if I let her.

"Mum . . . please. What's going on?"

"Kirby . . ." She stopped and put her hands to her face, pressing them against her cheeks in that scary holding-everything-together way.

"Mum!" I got up, but she held up a hand.

"I'm all right. I'm okay. It's just that I've got to tell you and . . ."

My body went cold. "Tell me what?"

She brought her hands down and said, "I'm so sorry. I've made a botch of this."

Tell me something I didn't know. "It's okay, Mum. We can go back. The hospital will . . ."

She cut me off. "You don't understand, darling. I can't go back. I can't do that anymore. I can't . . ." She stopped and took a shuddering breath. I felt sickness through to my bones. What was happening? What wasn't she telling me?

I soon found out.

She took my hands. "I've been such a bad mother to you."

I broke in, squeezing her fingers hard. "You haven't. You *haven't*. I don't want an ordinary mother. You're great!"

She managed a smile, but it faded so quickly, I might have imagined it. "I have to go away. That's what I'm trying to tell you. I have to go to Africa. That's where I'll be working."

The words hung in the hot air. Africa? She was going to Africa?

"What about—" I cleared my throat and tried again. "What about me?"

"My brother has offered to have you."

"Your brother? You've got a brother?" I stared at her. Nothing was sinking in.

"I've got five brothers." I was still taking that in when she added, "And three sisters."

My mind couldn't deal with that right now. "Mum! You can't go and leave me! With people I don't know! With strangers!"

Her fingers fluttered against my grip. "My brother Caleb. He's your uncle. He said . . . he said they'll look after you. You'll be part of a family, a real family. Naomi knows how to be a mother. Not like me." She talked fast, convincing herself.

I snatched my hand away. "I won't go! You're crazy!"

Her head drooped. "Sometimes I think so." I stared at her, too horrified to say anything. "The only thing I know for sure is that I want what's right for you." She swallowed and gasped in a breath to whisper, "And this is right. I love you, and I know this is what has to be."

I jumped up and stumbled around the room. She came and put her arms around me; but that scared me even more, because every muscle in her body vibrated with tension. "It won't be forever. I promise you that."

"I'll stay with Gemma. Louisa will have me." Anything rather than go to strangers.

She answered me in a voice she'd dragged up from the depths. "They can't afford it. And I can't pay her. I only get a living allowance in Africa."

I broke away, too stunned to think. This was my life. She couldn't do this to me.

I wanted to shake her and pound her and hit her, but I was scared if I touched her she'd fly into pieces. She seemed to be holding herself together by sheer willpower. She couldn't be doing this to me, not my mother. My mother would never do such a horrible thing. Except that she was.

"This brother. Why haven't you told me about him and all the others?" My voice was high and thin. "Why did you say we've got no relatives?" I stamped my foot and kicked the settee. "Why, Mum?"

At last she whispered, "He's religious. They all are. They're called the Children of the Faith. They threw me out when I was sixteen because I . . . because . . ." She gulped and then finished in that flat, dead voice, "Because."

"Mum!" I shrieked. "You can't leave me with them! A bunch of nutters! You're crazy! I'll run away! I don't believe all this!"

She lifted her head and gave me a brief look and her eyes were dark and desperate. "You must go to them, Kirby. It won't be for long. It'll be for the best. I don't want you to end up like me. No good for anything."

"Mum!" But this time I whispered it. "Oh, Mum, don't do this! Don't say things like that!"

She shook her head, waving it backward and forward until I wanted to grab it and make her keep it still. "I don't want you to end up feeling empty. I don't want you to end up having to run and run because you're too scared to keep still. Caleb said they'll care for you. He's promised they'll love you and care for you and . . ."

"You've *seen* him? You've *talked* to him? Already?" How could she do this? And not tell me? Then I remembered. "He was one of those creepy guys who came to the flat! Wasn't he?" She didn't need to answer.

It was a nightmare. How could my whole life have spun out of control in three short days? I shouted at Mum, I begged her, I cried. Every word made her wince and shudder, but she just kept repeating, *It won't be for long* and *It's for the best*. The meal I'd eaten churned in my stomach, and I could taste the grease in my mouth. If only she'd talk to me, explain things.

The room I was in had no meaning, there was nothing familiar to hold on to. I went outside and put my hand on the heap, leaned my arms on the roof and lay my cheek against the cool metal. Night had come, but I hadn't noticed. Traffic sped past on the road. There were people everywhere, but there was nobody I could talk to. Not even my mother. I went back inside. "Mum?"

"It's for the best, Kirby. I want the best for you. I love you."

I shouted at her, argued, yelled and screamed for hours. She just looked at me with her desperate, empty eyes and kept repeating that this was the best thing she could do for me. It didn't convince me, and I don't think it convinced her, but she wouldn't, or couldn't, tell me why.

There was a clock with red digits, and I noticed it click over: 2:43 A.M. "You don't love me," I whispered.

This time the words were different. I had to hold my breath to hear what she said. "I do. I do love you. But loving is so hard when you don't love yourself."

I gave up then. Terror clawed at my throat and chest. She'd already gone away and left me and no matter what I tried, I wasn't going to be able to bring her back. I was alone, and it was no use crying for Louisa, who was too far away and too poor to help me.

"When do you go?" My voice sounded dead in my ears.

"Tomorrow." She glanced at the red eyes of the clock. "Today." The word sank like lead through the stuffy air.

I curled up on a bed. I was cold, shivering in the hot night. My mother was abandoning me, and there was nothing I could do about it. She'd been clever. If Lousia had known about her plans, she'd have taken me in and just made the money stretch. So Mum had made up the moving to Wellington bit. She knew I couldn't go rushing back to Louisa without money.

"How long are you going for?" I asked, my voice muffled in the bedspread. Two weeks? I could maybe survive two weeks.

"A month or two. Maybe three. I don't know yet."

I believe that my heart stopped beating, and I fiercely wished it hadn't started again. "You can't do this," I cried, but my voice came out in a whimper.

"They'll be good to you." She sounded like somebody reciting a lesson. "Your uncle Caleb will be a father to you. He was always kind, kinder than—I loved him. You'll have brothers and sisters. You've missed out on so much, living with me."

"I haven't missed anything!" I yelled. "They're religious! They'll turn me into a freak!"

"They'll give you a real family."

I stared at her, searching for words, searching for the key that would bring her back to me. But there were no words. There was nothing. She had gone from me as surely as if she'd already boarded the plane for Africa.

My uncle Caleb Pilgrim came at eight o'clock in the morning. I must have slept, because it was his knock on the door that woke me. He walked into the motel unit and glanced around. I'd never seen such a gray man. His hair was gray, his clothes were gray, his shoes were gray. I couldn't see his eyes— they were lost under a frown and wrinkles. Mum and I must've got our wild dark hair and our big brown eyes from a different strand of the gene pool.

He went up to Mum and kissed her forehead. "This is a godly thing you are doing, Martha."

"Her name's Ellen," I said, sitting up. I pushed at my hair and held it back out of my eyes so I could look at him.

He stared down at me. I was watching for disapproval, the telltale tightening of the mouth, a frown. Anything. His expression didn't change, not even by one muscle twitch. "She was baptized Martha." He stopped looking at me and gave Mum the benefit of his gray stare. "My prayers have been answered. Martha is back among the Chosen Ones doing the work of the Lord, and she has commended the care of her child into my hands."

I looked at Mum—tried to catch her eye. If she just lifted an eyebrow and turned her mouth down and shrugged, then I'd know I wasn't going mad. I'd know all this was a crazy movie we'd walked into and could walk out of again. But Mum didn't know the script. She was looking as if he'd beaten her. She stood beside the stove, rubbing it with a tea towel.

"Mum?" I went over to her. "You've got to tell me what's wrong! You've got to tell me why!"

The gray man spoke. "There is nothing wrong, child. Your mother has repented and is making atonement for her years of sin."

His words skidded across the top of my consciousness. I concentrated on trying to reach Mum, break her out of her hideous shell.

"Mum?"

She put her arms around me then and hugged the breath out of me. "I have to do this," she said. "I have to go." She rubbed her cheek against my hair. "It is for the best, Kirby. For both of us."

I wrenched myself out of her arms. My uncle was in the way. I remember banging into him, then I was standing up against the wall. It was made of concrete blocks and painted white. It felt rough and cold against my T-shirt. "I'll never forgive you! Never! How can you do this to me? How can you abandon your own child? You always said you loved me. You always said I meant more to you than anything, but it's a lie, isn't it? A goddamned filthy lie! I hate you! Get out of my life!"

She looked as if I'd punched her—shocked and white and broken. My uncle said something, but I didn't hear it. I was waiting for Mum to come to me and tell me everything was all right. To tell me she did love me and we'd go back home, where I'd look after her again and Louisa would look after me.

She didn't. She just took a huge, ragged breath, lifted up her hands, and plaited her hair into a single tight braid. She twisted a band onto the end of it—a band she'd brought without my having to remind her. She never tied her hair back. "I am ready, Caleb," she whispered. She came over to me, kissed me with cold lips, and whispered, "I do love you. I do. Never forget it." Then she picked up two of her bags and walked out the door.

I listened for a long time, listened until the noise of Uncle Caleb's car got mixed up with the cars on the road outside the motel. Cars have a gray sound. I never knew that before.

I didn't know I was crying until I rubbed my chest and discovered that my T-shirt was wet. How could I be crying when I wasn't making any noise? My throat hurt as if somebody was pulling a drawstring around it. The stippled roughness of the concrete wall was still against my back.

I heard the door open and turned my head. "Mum?" But it was only a strange boy. I did hear myself then. I shrieked and wailed and carried on like a hurricane. He sat in a chair, and I suppose he watched me. He certainly didn't say anything.

"Get out," I managed to say when there didn't seem to be any tears left.

He was using the wrong script too. "I am Daniel. Your cousin."

"I don't care if you're the devil himself! Get the hell out of here!" That should shock him and make him run for Daddy, and then Uncle Caleb would beat me and I could kick him and swear and pull his hair and do all the things I wanted to do to my mother.

I don't remember a lot about what happened after that. There are bits that stick in my head like clear pictures, as if somebody had paused the video. Daniel handed me a drink, and I threw it across the room. I see the glass traveling through the air and milk spilling out of it in an arc. I see him sitting quite still in the orange chair, his hand ready to turn another page in the Bible he was reading. I see him holding out a folded white handkerchief to me.

Uncle Caleb came back at some point. The pair

of them got down on their knees and prayed. They were praying for Mum and for me—Martha's child, they called me. "Goddamn leave me out of your goddamn prayers!" I yelled, and then I was crying again.

I'm pretty ashamed of how I behaved when I look back on it all now. I guess it was the suddenness of it that got to me. Actually, Uncle Caleb was quite kind in his own way. He just let me rant and rave, and he or Daniel cleaned up the mess when I screamed at them and threw my food at the wall. He let me yell and chuck things all that day, and then when I started again the next day, he put his hand on my head and said, "That is enough, child. It is time to get on with life. Go and have a shower." And I did, just like that.

We had to be out of the motel by ten o'clock. Daniel put my bags in the back of a station wagon. "Do you want to ride in the front?"

I shook my head. I wanted to sleep. I crawled in and lay down on the backseat. Uncle Caleb made me sit up and put the seat belt on. The car moved off. Daniel was driving. He drove better than Mum did, or it might have been that this was a better car than the heap. What had happened to the heap?

I stared at the back of Daniel's head. He was out of the ark. Bad haircut. White shirt. Long trousers and shoes and socks. In this weather. The sun burned in on me and I went to sleep. When I woke up, the car had stopped and Uncle Caleb was opening the door. "We are home, child. Come and meet your new family."

Child. I had a name, why couldn't he use it? He'd never once called me by my name. Neither had Daniel. "Kirby," I muttered. "My name is Kirby." I struggled out, not feeling exactly in the mood for being paraded in front of all the cousins.

They were standing in a group on the veranda. I didn't want to look at them, so I looked at the house instead. Wooden, painted white. Blue windowsills, gray roof.

Uncle Caleb said something. I turned my head and stared at him. Had he spoken in English? Nothing made sense. He took my arm and steered me inside. Again, I couldn't look at the people when they followed me in. Big room. Kitchen at one end, fireplace at the other. Wooden polished floors. Rugs. A lot of religion on the walls.

More words, but I couldn't shut them out this time. "This is your aunt Naomi."

My aunt Naomi put her hands on my shoulders,

leaned forward, and kissed me on both cheeks. "We welcome you to our family, niece." I swallowed and tried to say something. She was quite tall, and she smelled of lavender and sweat. Her hair was a faded blond color and pulled back into a long plait that hung down her back. She would've been quite pretty if she'd had a decent haircut. The long skirt and apron she wore didn't hide the fact that she was pregnant.

Uncle Caleb went on with the introductions. "Daniel you have already met. He is the eldest. Rachel, Rebecca—welcome your new sister." Two girls came up and kissed me the same way my aunt had done. They were twins and about the same age as Gemma's younger brother, around twelve, I guessed. "Welcome," they murmured. They were fine boned, with long, fair hair, and their eyes were huge and wary.

The next in line was a boy. "Abraham," his father said. Bad haircut, just like Daniel's. He didn't kiss me, but stood in front of me and gave a sort of bow. His eyes were big like his sisters', but there was nothing wary about them. He screwed up his mouth and flicked his eyebrows. The others all looked sort of holy. Not Abraham.

"Luke," said my uncle, putting his hand on the shoulder of the smallest boy. "Welcome," he said, shyly. Then words burst out as if he couldn't stop them. "I'm seven, how old are you?"

Before I could even think about trying to get my voice working, his father had quelled him with a glance. Luke hung his head and shuffled nearer Abraham. The children all seemed to hold their breath. Abraham glanced swiftly at his father, but Caleb took the hand of his youngest daughter and said, "This is Magdalene, who was five the day before yesterday." The day they'd come for me. Magdalene sent one scared glance at me, then bent her head so that all I could see was her blond hair scraped back into the hideous plait all the girls wore. Caleb swept his gray glance around his family. "I want you to welcome Esther, your new sister."

I gasped. *Esther?* "I am not Esther," I said, keeping my teeth together so I wouldn't yell. "My name is Kirby."

Aunt Naomi said, "The women of our faith all have biblical names. As do the men." She smoothed back my wild hair and smiled at me. "We have given you the name Esther."

I stared at her. She was so different from Mum.

Her face looked polished, no makeup, and she didn't pluck her eyebrows. Her clothes were unbelievable. A long skirt. Dark brown. A blouse, long-sleeved and white, done up to the neck and down to the wrists. Big white apron. Shoes and stockings. I turned my head to look at my cousins. Rachel and Rebecca wore stuff exactly like their mother, but their skirts were blue and they wore socks instead of stockings. They all had braids. Something jolted in my head. Before Mum left, she had pulled her hair into a braid.

I looked at them, standing there watching me. I shook my head, twisting it from side to side. "I am not Esther," I repeated. "I'm Kirby."

Aunt Naomi took no notice. "Come with me, Esther. I will show you your room and help you change your clothes."

I hugged my arms around my T-shirt. It was my favorite one, black and shabby. "Wait!" I cried. "Can I watch the news? Please?" I needed to know if something terrible was happening where Mum was going.

"We do not have a televison," said my aunt.

"The radio, then," I said desperately. "Let me listen to the news!"

She smiled at me. "We do not have a radio or a newspaper. We keep our thoughts turned to the Lord."

I couldn't take it in. She took my arm and led me down a passage to a bedroom with two sets of bunks. "This is where the girls sleep." She walked to the bunks nearest the door and put her hand on the top one. "This is your bed. And these are your clothes." She smiled at me. "I do hope they fit. We did not have a lot of warning of your coming, but the sisters have helped." I thought she meant Rachel and Rebecca, but then she added, "And the girls, of course."

She held up the white blouse and a long blue skirt. "I don't wear clothes like that," I said. "Where are my bags? I want my own clothes."

She took no notice. "Please get changed now, Esther. And plait your hair into a braid like mine."

She walked out and left me.

2

THE NEXT FEW DAYS DRAGGED past in a blur. I couldn't seem to keep my mind on anything. Mum might as well be dead. It would have been easier if she'd died, then I wouldn't have felt so betrayed. She'd chosen to do this. That's what I couldn't get my head around. I spent those days curled up on my bunk, and I wouldn't take off my shorts and T-shirt.

The twins whispered at their end of the room and underneath me in the bottom bunk; Magdalene cried herself to sleep each night. People came and went through the house, a lot of people one day. Rebecca murmured something about it being the Circle of Fellowship. Who cared?

Then the next morning, Aunt Naomi came in bright and early, and she didn't bring me my breakfast. "Today you get up and join the family, Esther. Have a shower and leave those clothes in the bathroom. Put on the ones we made for you." She whipped the blankets off me and yanked me out of the bunk.

I tumbled onto the floor. "I'm Kirby," I yelled. "I'm not Esther, for God's sake."

Wow, did the world ever explode around my ears then! I was hauled to my feet and marched out of the room. I kicked and screamed and bellowed, but she was strong. I'd never thought of a pregnant woman being strong. I'd never had anything to do with a pregnant woman before.

She opened a door and shoved me inside a room and let me fall in a heap on the polished floor. Uncle Caleb was sitting at a desk writing a letter. I jumped up. "Get your hands off me!"

Aunt Naomi didn't look at me. "Husband"—yes, she really did call him that—"this child has taken the name of the Lord in vain. She has committed the sin of blasphemy."

"I don't believe in God," I said.

Bad mistake. Oh, very bad mistake.

"Down on your knees," Uncle Caleb thundered. "Call the children," he ordered Aunt Naomi. They came at a rush, even little Magdalene, and they were all pulling on their dreary clothes.

And they prayed for me. At least, Uncle Caleb prayed and the others all said "Praise the Lord" after he'd been ranting and raving for a while, a bit like a chorus. My knees started to hurt. I sat down on my butt and glared at them. The kids and my aunt all had their eyes shut, but old loudmouth was watching me. I was expecting him to haul me up, and then I'd have belted him back, but he only prayed louder and got more personal. "Bring this wayward child, our daughter, into the path of righteousness. Show her the errors of her defiance *blah blah blah*. . . ."

I got up and walked out.

They stayed there. I went to the kitchen. There was a pot of something on the stove. Porridge? I ate some of the homemade bread with honey on it.

They were still in there.

I crept down the passage. Magdalene was crying again. I went back to the kitchen. The big clock on the wall—the only one in the house—said half past seven. I gritted my teeth. They'd have to stop soon.

Uncle Caleb would have to go to work.

I had a shower, wrapped the towel around me, and went to get clean clothes from my bag. It wasn't in my room. My knees gave way and I sank down onto some big cushions on the floor. All I owned in the world now was what I held in my hands: a T-shirt, shorts, and my underwear. I sat for a long time, staring at them. My mother had turned me into a refugee. At last, I got up and put them on. I brushed my hair, and discovered there was no mirror in the bedroom. I glided back to the bathroom. No mirror there, either. I tiptoed to the study door; they were still praying.

How long would my uncle keep them there? Aunt Naomi couldn't stay like that forever, she might have the baby. I sneaked a look. They were all still on their knees, and Magdalene was sobbing.

I went and sat on the veranda in the sun. I could leave. Go to the police.

I thought about it for a long time. Even walked to the gate. But it wouldn't work. They didn't beat me or starve me. I figured praying over me wasn't a crime that would get me away from them.

There was no one else I could go to and my uncle was the only person who knew where Mum was.

Nine o'clock. They still prayed.

I sat at the end of the hall and, in my head, swore every stinking swear word I could think of. One of the twins came out to go to the toilet, Rebecca, I think. I waited outside the toilet door. She whispered, "Run away, if you're going to. Otherwise we have to stay in there till you come back in. We stayed in there praying for two days before . . ." She stopped, then said, "Before Christmas."

She went back to the study.

I had nowhere to go. I sat on the veranda hugging my knees and rocking. *Mum, come back, I don't know what to do.*

But there wasn't any choice. Not now. When school started, I could talk to somebody. Make friends. Find somebody to run away to.

Until then I would have to be a godly child called Esther who wore horrible clothes, who didn't swear or take the name of the Lord in vain, and God knows what else.

I went back to the study. I stood outside the door. *I don't want to do this.*

I listened to the droning of my uncle. Praise the Lord. Magdalene hiccuped. The poor kid was only five! I could see her through the gap in the door,

35

kneeling all by herself, tears tracking down her face. It made me angry, and because of that I grabbed hold of enough courage to go back in.

I took a deep breath, pulled the door wide, and stalked into the room. I knelt down on the hard floor and clamped my mouth and my eyes shut so that I wouldn't yell and I couldn't cry.

Magdalene gasped and sobbed harder. There was a stirring and almost a sighing, but nobody picked her up or put an arm around her.

I hate them. *I hate them all. Goddamn them all to hell. Except Magdalene.*

I reckon it was another half hour before Uncle Caleb let up. By then my knees were numb, and I was raging mad, which was better than wanting to howl my eyes out.

"Praise the Lord! Praise the Lord!"

There was a sighing around the room, and they stood up. I sat back on my heels and watched Aunt Naomi shut her eyes for a second and rub her back.

It's not my fault, you stupid cow.

Uncle Caleb eyed me sternly. "Get to your feet, Esther. Never grieve the Lord again with your blasphemy or your disobedience. You are a child of God. Go and change your clothes."

My knees hurt. I lifted my head. "My name is Kirby," I said. "I am not Esther."

Magdalene gave another sob and then slapped her hands over her mouth. I couldn't stand the way nobody tried to comfort her. I held out my arms. "Come along, princess. Come and show me how to get into these funny clothes. I've never worn a skirt in my life."

She stared at me for three whole seconds before she threw herself into my arms and clung to me as if she was scared I'd vanish into thin air. I hugged her back. I could relate to that feeling.

Aunt Naomi touched my shoulder. "That is kind of you, Esther. But please do not call her 'princess' again. We do not recognize the monarchy."

So why doesn't that surprise me? "I am not Esther," I said and carried Magdalene off to the bedroom.

I plonked her on the desk under the window and picked up the dreary clothes. I clowned around and made her laugh, trying to put the underpants on my head and the skirt around my neck. It was lucky she was there, and it was lucky she needed cheering up, or I would've killed somebody, or broken something or—the really big one—I might have said some naughty words. They actually wore this stuff? *I* had to wear this stuff, too? The underpants were unreal. Big enough to hide a cow in, and the stuff you make kids' pajamas out of. I pushed them under my pillow along with the petticoat. I left the two top buttons of the blouse undone. The skirt didn't have buttons; it had a slit at each side and tied at the waist with tapes.

Holy cow. Was that blasphemy? No doubt I'd find out, since it's one of the things I say a lot.

Magdalene smiled at me and chuckled. She looked happy for a split second. Then she said, "Are you going to die, too?"

"Not till I'm a hundred and three," I said, picking her up and throwing her in the air. "Why? Who else died?"

"Miriam." She ducked her head in my shoulder and wouldn't say any more.

I carried her out to the family room, the heavy material dragging around my knees and ankles. So who was Miriam? When had she died? What of?

I opened my mouth to ask Aunt Naomi, but she got in first. "That is better. The clothes fit well." She tweaked at the skirt, then fastened the two top buttons of my blouse. "We wear the blouse buttoned at the neck and the wrists," she said.

I tugged at the collar. "But it's so hot!"

She smiled at me, "You will soon get used to it. You would not wish to dress in an unseemly way."

I opened my mouth to argue, but she pointed at a basket of wet washing. "Hang out the washing, please, Esther, and when you have done that, pick some peas for dinner."

Esther. I opened my mouth, but Magdalene was staring at me, terrified. I shut it and picked up the cane basket.

I'd never hung out washing. Our flat didn't have a clothesline, so we used the dryer. Magdalene showed me how to do it. She showed me how to pick peas, too. That was after I'd pulled the first plant out by the roots. We ate quite a few, and Magdalene giggled a lot. Both those things had to be healthy, I reckoned. I started calling her "Maggie," and she giggled harder.

It kept me from thinking about Mum.

Uncle Caleb arrived home at ten past twelve for lunch—which was a revelation. Lunch, I mean, not him arriving home. It started off with grace. Not the "Bless this bunch as they crunch their lunch" sort. Oh no, this was full on and serious. Five minutes at least and filled with *Praise the Lord*s. Then we sat down.

I ate a sandwich made from thick slices of homemade bread and filled with homegrown lettuce and tomato. I'd just poured a glass of water when I accidentally let loose another hurricane.

"Who was Miriam?" I asked.

Everyone just stopped. I swear there wasn't a sound in that room, even the clock stopped ticking. I looked around. Uncle Caleb—face tight, gray tinged with red. Aunt Naomi, face hard, lips shut tight. Daniel not looking at anyone, eyes on his plate. Rachel staring at the ceiling. Rebecca, lips pinched shut over a bad taste. Abraham shot a glance at his father, then kept his eyes on the table. Luke and Maggie had their mouths open, and their eyes were frightened.

"Leave the table," Uncle Caleb snapped.

"Why?" My voice went high and squeaky. "Uncle Caleb, that's not fair! What have I done wrong?"

None of my cousins looked at me, except Maggie, and she had her hands over her mouth and tears were filling her eyes. "Leave the table," my uncle repeated in a voice cold enough to freeze over hell.

I jumped up. "No! I won't!" I thumped my fist on the snowy white cloth. "You're not fair! First you change my name! Then you make me wear these stinking clothes! And now when I ask something perfectly reasonable you throw a fit!"

A silence sank over the room, terrible and suffocating. I wanted to run, but I was damned if I'd give him the satisfaction, so I stayed there with my heart hammering its way out of my rib cage.

He picked up his knife and fork and put them together in an exactly straight line down the middle of his plate. "Miriam was our daughter. She died four weeks ago. Now leave the table. Go to your room and braid your hair in a godly manner."

What did she die of? Where are the photos of her? Why don't you talk about her? But the questions died on my lips.

I went slowly to the bedroom. Daniel was seventeen, and the twins were twelve. Did she come in the gap between? She'd be my age or perhaps a bit older. Or perhaps she'd come in the gap between Maggie and the new baby. Why wouldn't they talk about her? I'd make them. It wasn't good to keep things bottled up. Then I remembered Mum. My darling mother who told me everything—except the

41

things she didn't want me to know. She had grown up in this weird faith.

I shook my head. Don't think about her. I shut out too, the feelings spiraling around—hurt, loneliness. Hot, raging fury.

Aunt Naomi came in after about ten minutes. "I'm sorry about Miriam," I said, not because I was trying to find out anything, but because I was sorry.

She picked up my hairbrush. "We do not talk about her," was all she said, and then she attacked my hair as if it was a poisonous snake. She yanked it back and then plaited it into the tightest plait in the world. I let her do it, then I hauled the band off it and ran my fingers through it to undo it. "I don't wear my hair like that."

She slapped the brush back in my hand. "Fix it. Then you can take the little ones to the park for the afternoon."

Get out of this house for a few hours? Yes! I braided my hair and went to get Abraham, Luke, and Maggie. Maggie had a scarf over her hair. Aunt Naomi handed me one as well. "Women of our faith wear their hair covered in public."

I took the scarf. I covered my hair with it. "Where's the park?"

She told me. Weird, I didn't even know which part of the country I was in. I asked her. Wanganui.

The twins were helping Aunt Naomi bottle plums and watched us as we walked out the door. Daniel had gone back to work with Uncle Caleb.

The day was hot. I took off the scarf and undid my hair the second we turned the corner away from the house. "Miriam never did that," Abraham said, then stopped in a hurry. So Miriam must've been old enough to take them to the park. She must've been in the Daniel–twins gap. About my age or maybe a bit older.

I touched Abraham's shoulder to get him moving again. "I'm sorry Miriam died. Was she nice?"

But they wouldn't talk about her, not even Abraham, with his bold eyes. Maggie's hand crept into mine. "She used to tell me stories," she whispered.

We got to the park. There was a fountain, all cool and splashing. I took off the god-awful shoes and socks and sat on the edge, my feet in the water.

"We're not allowed to do that," Luke said, his hand splashing at the water.

"So don't, then."

The pair of them stared at me, then Abraham let out a yell and jumped in beside me, emptying half the water over me. Luke, with a scared look over his shoulder, slid in beside him. I pulled Maggie's shoes off and she sat beside me, swinging her feet in the water. I'd probably get prayed over when I got them home. I didn't care, there was too much on my mind. There had to be a reason for what Mum had done. It wasn't because she'd stopped loving me. My head knew that even if it wasn't how I felt. So why?

I knew so little. She'd left home on her sixteenth birthday. She said she couldn't stand it any longer. God, could I ever believe that. And she said her father belted them. At least Uncle Caleb didn't seem to be into physical violence.

I went over what else I knew of Mum's life, but there wasn't much. I was born when she was twenty-six. My father died of leukemia when I was four, but she said the marriage wouldn't have lasted because he couldn't stand her flakiness.

How was I going to survive living with the Pilgrim family for days, let alone months? I wanted to cry and hide my head in my horrible scarf.

"You will hurt your fingers, Esther," Maggie whispered, timidly putting a hand over mine where I'd twisted the scarf tight.

I glanced at her worried face and took a deep

breath. I said something flippant so that she smiled. The boys jumped out of the water and raced over to a climbing frame. Maggie and I sat on, our feet cool in the water. "I'm going to find out why she left," I murmured. "And I'm going to get her back."

Maggie stared at me. "It's okay, kiddo," I said. "I haven't lost my marbles. Come on, I'll give you a swing."

I suddenly felt better. I wouldn't accept this, shrug my shoulders, and get on with it the way we always did with problems. I shoved hard at the swing; they weren't going to change me.

We went home, with the boys wet to their skins. Aunt Naomi frowned and lectured me. The boys were sent to change, and I had to help cook dinner. I had to make a plum pudding with a sponge top. I looked at the recipe book she'd given me.

"I don't know how to do this," I said. "What does it mean, 'Cream the butter and sugar'?"

The twins stifled giggles, my aunt shook her head as if she couldn't believe a girl of my age could be so lacking in the basic skills of living, but she showed me how to beat them together. She didn't have an electric beater.

Rebecca was doing the ironing, and Rachel was

kneading bread dough. There was an embroidered text on the wall that said THE DEVIL FINDS WORK FOR IDLE HANDS. When Uncle Caleb and Daniel came home, my uncle sat at the kitchen table and asked, "Wife, have the children upheld the Rule, this day?"

Maggie was sitting at the table shelling peas and she whimpered. I grinned at her, but my heart was beating faster, and that made me mad. I would be me, not some dorky drip called Esther. Aunt Naomi told him how I'd brought the boys home soaking wet.

He didn't look at me, just told us all to go to his study. I hoped the dinner would burn. We knelt, and I suppose they all shut their eyes, but I didn't, although I bowed my head so Uncle Caleb couldn't see that my eyes were open.

I tried not to listen, but couldn't help it. He went on about how my lack of discipline was a sad lapse and how with the help of the Lord I would learn to uphold the Rule so as not to grieve the Lord. I learned during that session that this stupid Rule they kept on about meant you couldn't do anything a normal kid would do.

"Help our beloved daughter Esther to guard her tongue so that her speech may be seemly. Help her to speak without shortening her words. Help her to be godly."

"Praise the Lord."

"Help our beloved daughter Esther to discipline her thoughts and deeds. Help her to set an example of godliness and seemliness that the younger children may learn by her example."

"Praise the Lord."

My knees were burning, I clenched my jaw shut, and my fingernails dug into the palms of my hands.

The Lord was going to be busy. He had to help me be modest, unassuming, dutiful, obedient, chaste. He had to help me keep my thoughts on Him. I wasn't to be selfish and consider my own wishes and desires.

"That is all, family. Go about your duties."

"Holy cow," I breathed.

Uncle Caleb heard. Down we went for another ten everlasting minutes. My state of mind was not exactly calm, holy, or reverent. But I kept my mouth shut. Just as well he couldn't read my mind.

The dinner didn't burn. I reckon Aunt Naomi had it planned so she could leave it while we prayed.

Mum, why did you abandon me? Why did you turn me into a refugee?

After dinner and after prayers that night I asked Aunt Naomi, "Please, Aunt, could I look at my mother's luggage?" She'd only taken two bags to Africa—the rest of them had to be here somewhere. There probably wouldn't be any clues in her stuff, but it was somewhere to start looking.

"It is nothing to do with me," said Aunt Naomi, so I took a deep breath and asked my uncle.

"It is nothing to do with you," he said, and he was just as closed off and determined as Mum had been when she wouldn't tell me anything. If I argued with him, he'd probably haul everyone into his study for another prayer session.

Daniel might tell me something. I managed to ask him when I went out to pick some sweet corn for tea the next afternoon. He was weeding along a row of carrots. "Daniel, do you know what happened to Mum's gear?"

He sat back on his heels and stared at me. "My father does not want you to have it."

"It isn't his. And I don't want to have it. I just want to look through it."

He stared at me some more. I'd dumped a weighty problem on him. "It is in the garage," he said at last. "In the cupboard beside the workbench."

I could've hugged him. "Thanks, Daniel!"

The next problem was, when could I look through it? Aunt Naomi kept me busy all day. She was horrified that I couldn't cook, or clean a stove, or iron the ghastly blouses properly. Maggie was my constant companion. If it hadn't been for her, I'd have gone bananas, but she seemed to need me. She grew anxious if I disappeared somewhere and she didn't know. Miriam. She thought I was going to die like Miriam.

After worrying the problem around in my head for hours, I came to the conclusion the only time to look at Mum's stuff was the middle of the night. I took the flashlight from the laundry while I was folding the daily washing. "Mum, you'd be stunned if you could see me now," I muttered, folding my spare skirt and blouse, both exactly the same colors as the lot I was wearing.

That evening I put the littlies to bed. Abraham and Luke bounced and yelled and had a pillow fight. Uncle Caleb stormed in and killed it dead. "You will teach them discipline," he said coldly.

"Yes, Uncle Caleb." An idea hit me. "Uncle Caleb . . . could I read to them? Where are the books?"

"You may read the Bible," he said. His mouth

twitched into what could have been an approving smile.

"Yes, all right . . . but other stories too. Where are they?" I looked around the room, but the only books were a Bible by each bed.

"We do not believe in stories and novels," he said. "The word of the Lord is sufficient."

So what did they do in their spare time with no television, no radio, and no books? Play cards? Strip poker, maybe? I think not.

I took Maggie into our room and tucked her into bed. "Tell me a story," she whispered as I hugged her.

"Like Miriam did?" I asked, and felt her nod. "I'll tell you about my mother, and you tell me about Miriam." She nodded again, so I told her about Mum and me dying our hair for Christmas, and I managed not to cry. "Your turn," I said.

She reached up and touched my hair. "She had pretty hair. Yellow and straight. Not like yours." And that was it, she just turned over then and snuggled down. I went back to tuck the boys in. "Tell us a story," Abraham whispered, his eyes sparkling.

"Come down here, then," I said, and moved over so there was room for him beside me on Luke's bunk. I told them the story of the Three Billy Goats

Gruff and we all went *"Trip-trap, trip-trap.* Who's going over MY bridge?" together in a whisper muffled by the blankets. They loved it.

I looked in on Maggie before I went back to the family room. She was sleeping, and there were no tear tracks down her cheeks.

"Is she crying?" Aunt Naomi asked.

I shook my head and she relaxed. "Good. You are good with her." It was the nearest to approval that I'd got since I'd arrived in this house a whole huge long week ago. To reward me, she gave me a basket of mending. I'm sure knowing how to sew buttons on is an essential life skill I will one day be very glad I have. Not.

I went to bed, planning to stay awake and creep out when everyone was asleep, but I fell asleep and didn't wake up until Aunt Naomi called me at seven.

It was Sunday, and we went to church at ten o'clock. I kept my head down. I didn't want to be part of this crowd of people in their stupid clothes and their stupider ideas. But I couldn't shut my ears. All around me people were greeting each other, chatting and laughing as they made their way into the hall. That went on for maybe half an hour with me feeling totally removed from it all, when suddenly they stopped talking and moved to their seats.

I glanced up, trying to see who had given the signal. It must've been the old guy now standing on the stage behind the lectern. He turned out to be the leader, his name was Ezra Faithful, and he did a great line in hellfire and damnation. He didn't seem to like women much, and I wanted to hit him.

After church they all stayed in the hall while girls spread food out in another room. I went outside and sat on the steps. Daniel followed me. "My father says you must come inside and eat the fellowship meal."

I shook my head. "Tell him to get stuffed. I want my mother."

"He will pray for you when we get home if you do not come," Daniel said. He held out his hand. "Come, Kirby. Sometimes it is easier to do what they say."

I was stunned. He had called me Kirby and he'd said . . . I'd think about that later. I got up and went with him.

I couldn't believe the meal. We had the grace—of course—and then we ate. But they were all so happy and joyful, just like one huge happy family. It turned my stomach, and I noticed that the happy, joyful men got served first by their wives, then the boys got served, while the women and girls helped themselves to anything that was left over.

Daniel handed me a plate of cold meat. "Don't strain yourself," I muttered.

Aunt Naomi put some of it on my plate. "Eat, Esther. It is a long time until dinner."

I kept my head down so I wouldn't have to look at anything or anyone. I knew they were looking at me, but whenever I caught somebody's eye they just smiled and murmured, "Welcome, Esther. You are welcome."

At home that evening, while I was clearing the table after dinner, I said, "Aunt Naomi, has my mother written to you?" Every day I hoped for a letter but they didn't even have a letter box.

"You must ask your uncle, Esther."

She *had* written, and they hadn't told me? "May I go now?" I was learning the rules of this place.

She nodded. "He is in his study."

I knocked on the door, waited until he said to come in. "Yes, Esther?"

"Has my mother written?"

"It is too soon to hear from her, Esther."

"May I write to her, then? Can I have her address? Please! I miss her so much!" I need to tell her how I'm going mad and that she has to come home.

"She is doing the Lord's work, Esther. You should rejoice." He bent to his Bible again. "You may write. I will address it for you, there is no need for you to have her address. I will post it for you."

Yeah, after you've read it first, you ugly, stinking old rat of a pig's bum! I went back to the family room too angry and upset to watch where I was going and slammed straight into the open door. The socks I darned had to be done again, I pulled the stitches so tight. I got told off for being wasteful of time, effort, and wool. The twins sat and sewed neat stitches into pictures for their bedroom wall. Not pictures, verses from the Bible. I stared at Rebecca's.

IF I TAKE THE WINGS OF THE MORNING AND

DWELL IN THE UTTERMOST PARTS OF THE SEA,

She was halfway through what could possibly turn out to be a *V*.

I hoped they'd jab themselves and fall asleep for a hundred years. Tonight I would stay awake, tonight I would search through Mum's stuff. There had to be a clue there somewhere.

The flashlight was a lump under my pillow when I went to bed. The house fell quiet around me. I waited for ages, and then I got up very carefully, slipped onto the floor, and went to the window.

It was an old house, and the windows slid up. There was a clanging noise in the wall from the weights or something. I sat on the sill, one leg dangling, and held my breath, listening. Nothing moved, and there was no sound except for my thudding heart.

There was a flower garden under the window. I pushed myself out from the sill and jumped so I landed clear of it. The grass was cool and crisp under my feet. I tiptoed to the garage, fumbling for the key under a loose brick in the path.

I turned it in the lock. Turned the door handle. No sound except my raspy breathing. Uncle Caleb would kill me. His God would strike me dead.

I found the cupboard. The bags were there, stacked neatly on a wide shelf. I took down the first one. It was one of those ones with handles and zips. I undid it carefully and lifted the stuff out. Mum's winter clothes. Her thick jerseys, skirts, a scarf. I lifted up the sweatshirt she'd always worn around home and held it against my face. It brought her back so sharply it hurt. I hugged it. *Mum, come back. How could you leave me?*

"You wicked, disobedient girl!"

I jumped a thousand feet. Uncle Caleb on the warpath. I stayed where I was, crouched on the floor holding my mother's sweatshirt in my arms. I said nothing. There was no point, and I fiercely didn't want him to know I was crying.

"How did you know where to look?" he thundered.

I sniffed, wiped my face on the sweatshirt, and looked all the way up to his gray face. *Daniel told me.* Daniel didn't deserve to be dropped in it. "It seemed the obvious place," I muttered.

He loomed above me. "I told you these things do not concern you."

Fury raged in me, chasing away the tears, and I was bloody glad of it. I jumped up and glared at him. "Uncle Caleb! I have to try to find out why she left! I need to know why she went away and left me." I held the sweatshirt in my hands, in front of me like a shield.

"You are a very self-centered child, Esther."

No expression in his voice or face. "Your mother experienced salvation. She has gone to do the Lord's work. You should rejoice. Put those things away, then go to your bed." He turned and walked out.

That was it? No dragging everyone out of bed and praying over me? I'd got off? Somehow I doubted it.

Suddenly I felt very tired. I struggled to lift the bag back onto the shelf. But I kept the sweatshirt.

In the morning, Aunt Naomi woke me up at six o'clock. "Get dressed," she whispered. "You are to study the Bible today."

"What?" I hoped I was still asleep and dreaming.

"You are to study the Bible. In the discipline room." She frowned. "Our own children have not had to use the room since . . ." She stopped suddenly. "Hurry."

What had she been going to say?

I slid down from the bunk and climbed into my neatly folded clothes. I took my own underwear out from under my pillow. I rinsed it out every night and put it there. When it wore out, I wouldn't wear any.

Maggie was fast asleep. When she woke up, I'd be gone. Knowing this household, nobody would tell her I wasn't dead.

I sat down beside her and shook her awake.

"Maggie, listen. I got into trouble last night and I have to spend the day in the discipline room." Her eyes got huge in her pinched little face. I shook her gently. "It's okay! I'm not going to die. I'll still be here in the house, but I think I have to stay there all day."

She just stared at me, then at last she said, "Miriam went to the discipline room and then she died."

Shock ran through me. Had she killed herself? I hugged Maggie. "I promise I won't die!" I grabbed a pencil and paper from the desk. "Look, I'll draw you a picture."

"No!"

I've never heard anything more eerie. The hair prickled on my scalp, and the twins stirred in their sleep. Maggie's face had gone dead white, and she was shaking. I grabbed her and held her tight. "Look, it's okay, kid! All right! I won't draw anything. I promise." She couldn't read. What could I do? Write her a note, anyway? "Watch, Maggie! This is a letter. Will you remember what it says?"

I felt her head nod against my shoulder. "Great! Now watch." She turned her head slightly. I read it to her as I wrote: I *am in the D room. I am being sOOOO gOOOOd.*

I drew smiley faces in all the *O*s.

"Now if you get worried when you wake up, you look at that and remember I'm being an angel." I hugged her again. "See you, button nose."

That made her giggle. They didn't use nicknames in this family. Rebecca turned over in the top bunk and muttered in her sleep. Would she like it if I called her Bex, or Becky?

I made my bed and went out, blowing Maggie a kiss on the way. Another puzzle. Why had she freaked out about drawing a picture, for God's sake?

Aunt Naomi put three pieces of plain bread on the table beside a glass of water. "This is your breakfast. I will bring you more at lunchtime and dinnertime."

"Thank you," I said. "I bet Mum's refugees would be thrilled to have all this. I'll think of them and give thanks while I eat it."

That ought to slide the ground out from under her feet—and the wicked uncle's—when she told him.

But she smiled at me and said, "That is indeed a seemly thought."

Hell for breakfast.

"I will take you to the bathroom three times during the day. Your uncle has put the study you are to do on the table in the discipline room."

They were going to lock me in?

I ate my "breakfast" and then toddled off to the discipline room behind Aunt Naomi's swishing skirts. She opened the door next to my uncle's study. The room wasn't much bigger than a cupboard, with a little table in it. I sat down on the chair. There was no window, and the light fell on the table in a pool, leaving the corners in shadow. I'd go mad if they locked me in. But when I looked after she'd left, there didn't seem to be a lock on the door. I got up and turned the handle, pushing it open to make sure. So, I was here on trust.

I sat and thought about my alternatives. If I ran away, Maggie would be devastated. Where would I go? Auckland was a long way from Wanganui. And Uncle Caleb was the only one who knew Mum's address. The same old problems. Wait till school starts, Kirby. Be patient. Spend the time working out why Mum left the way she did. There has to be a reason.

I looked at the stuff on the table. It turned out that my Bible study was to learn a psalm, and apparently I had to find it first, because there were no page numbers given.

Well, this was a new experience, ratting around in a Bible. But I'm smart and I found it, all seventeen verses of it. And it wasn't your modern rubbish, either. This version was full of *thee* and *thou* and *thy*. "For great is thy mercy toward me: and thou hast delivered my soul from the lowest hell." I hadn't seen much mercy so far, only a lot of hell.

The next verse was even better, and I felt it was talking directly about Uncle Caleb. "O God, the proud are risen against me, and the assemblies of violent men have sought after my soul."

I planned my day. I would learn the psalm before lunch. I've never found it difficult to learn things by heart. Mum and I used to do it for fun. She said poetry was part of my heritage. I knew heaps of it. In the afternoon, I would work out my next move in my search for Mum.

I wrote the psalm out on a bit of the paper, and then I started learning. When I learn things, I stride around the room. I shout out like a town crier. I'm noisy.

I forgot Uncle Caleb had his office right next door.

The door of the discipline room flew open just as I was standing on the chair and yelling, "Preserve my soul, for I am holy."

"Silence!" he thundered. "What do you think you are doing?"

"I'm doing my Bible study," I said. "I always learn things like this."

His face went from gray to dark. I'll beat you at this game, I thought. "Uncle Caleb, isn't this just wonderful! The words! So beautiful! I'd never realized before, but then, I've never even opened a Bible before. Thank you!" I beamed at him, waving the paper around.

He actually smiled at me. "Our dearest prayers are being answered, Esther. God does indeed work in mysterious ways. Continue your study, child, but if you could moderate the volume until I leave for work, I would appreciate it."

He went out, and I was so gobsmacked, I plopped down in the chair. He really meant all this stuff. It mattered to him that I was turning out to be a godly woman. I felt a bit guilty, and that made me mad. He had no right to impose his wacky beliefs on me. No flaming right at all.

I sat at the table and wrote, *My name is Kirby. I am not Esther.* I was me. Not some robot they programmed.

I had the prayer or psalm or whatever it was

learned by lunchtime, but I decided I wouldn't tell anyone I could learn it that quickly, or next time I might get three times as much.

Daniel brought me "lunch." "Gee, thanks," I said. "Sure you can spare it?"

He put down the tray and pulled one of Aunt Naomi's big biscuits wrapped in waxed paper from his pocket. "The diet gets a bit monotonous in here."

"Thanks!" I looked at him as I munched. "How would you know?"

"I know twenty psalms off by heart."

"I'm impressed! How can one boy be that wicked?"

But he didn't tell me. Instead he said, "You did not tell my father that I told you where to find your mother's things."

"How do you know I didn't?"

He smiled slightly. "My father would have mentioned it to me."

Of course he would. And there would have been a family prayer session over it. "Why did you tell me where they were?"

He looked somewhere over my head. "Sometimes, I believe my father is not always right."

I stared at him. He was quite gutsy in his own

weird way. "How's Maggie?" I asked.

"Magdalene is a little quiet, but she started smiling when she heard you—er—speaking the psalm so loudly."

I grinned. I would let rip again a few times this afternoon, just to let her know I was still alive.

He went away, and Aunt Naomi came and let me go to the toilet; then I was on my own for the afternoon.

It was the longest afternoon of my life. I tried to think constructively about Mum, but I couldn't, and if I could've painted my thoughts, they'd have been dark red and black and they'd have been slashed onto the paper with thick, ugly strokes.

I hate her, I really hate her.

I'm so frightened.

3

I ATE MY THREE PIECES OF BREAD
for dinner. The smell of roast lamb drifted down the
passage. My stomach rumbled. I was allowed out for
family prayers after dinner. I was hungry and steam-
ing mad, which I decided was heaps better than
being frightened and miserable. They always had a
Bible reading in the evening, nine million prayers,
and a couple of hymns.

"You did not die," Maggie whispered.

Bloody hell.

I'd never joined in before, but I thought, why
not? I held Maggie's hand and raised my voice in
song. I sang loudly and cheerfully and just a bit out

of time and a bit out of tune. But I looked happy and holy. My uncle and aunt smiled encouragingly, the kids giggled, and Daniel actually raised an eyebrow at me and smiled.

I got to recite my psalm, which I did with great expression and one-hundred-percent correctness. Uncle Caleb gave me his version of a smile, "You speak the words with feeling, Esther."

Even so, I got sent back to the discipline room for the evening. I whispered to Maggie, "I'll put another message under your pillow when I come to bed." She didn't smile, but seemed to relax.

Back in the discipline room I wrote Maggie her message: *I am gOOd.*

This time, I drew little faces in the *O*s, with big round mouths so that they looked as if they were singing.

Then I wrote to Louisa and Gemma. I wrote about what it was like here and how miserable and worried I was about Mum.

I feel betrayed. You wouldn't dump a scraggy old cat the way she dumped me. I HATE her. She must've been crazy to leave me here. This is the most idiot religion. Half the time I don't believe it's for real, it's so unbelievable. I have to watch what I say all the time, because if I say something they don't like, the whole family gets hauled in, and they pray about me. It's bloody lucky they can't read my thoughts. They're trying to change me, but they won't. I won't let them. I'm going to keep on being me. Kirby. I won't be Esther, which is what they've changed my name to.

How could I send it? I had no stamp or envelope and my uncle would read it and tear it up and pray over me. I started again:

Dear Louisa and Gemma,
I have surprising news for you. Mum has gone to Africa to work with refugees, and I am staying with her brother, and his family. I was surprised to find she had a brother, but she hasn't seen him since she was sixteen. They live very holy lives and are teaching me lots of prayers and songs. I like the language of the Bible they use. My aunt made me new clothes, because the women in their faith always wear skirts.

My uncle has Mum's address, if you want to write to her. Write to me, I miss you heaps.
Love and hugs,
Kirby

*   *   *

Aunt Naomi smiled when she read it the next day.

"Your uncle will post it today, Esther," she promised.

Maggie didn't say anything about her message until we were making our beds after breakfast (a thing I'd never done in my life B.P.—Before Pilgrims).

"It made me laugh," she said. She smoothed her hand across the paper. "Miriam drew pictures."

"What did she draw?" I asked carefully.

"She drew me," Maggie whispered. "My father was very angry. She had to go to the discipline room. . . ." Her voice trailed away.

"Is that when she died?" I kept on making the bed. I didn't want to do anything to stop her talking.

"Yes. She drew my picture and then she went to the discipline room and then we went to the study for two days and then she died."

I couldn't stand it. I threw my arms around her and held her tight as she sobbed and sobbed. "It isn't your fault she died," I cried. "She would have been very glad she was able to draw you before she died. She loved you." And why somebody didn't talk to this poor little kid about her dead sister was more than I could figure. It was criminal and totally not Christian. But I couldn't help wondering how she'd died, and the thought that I couldn't get out of my head was that she must have committed suicide.

I took the little ones to the park in the afternoon, my scarf coming off the second we turned the corner away from the house. I changed the route we took, so we could walk past a dairy. The only way I could think of to find out what was happening in the world was to read the newspaper billboards. Today's had an earthquake, but it wasn't in Africa.

I made the boys take off their shirts and god-awful trousers when they played in the water. Luke gasped, but Abraham ripped his clothes off and jumped in, so Luke followed. Maggie just wanted to sit beside me with her bare feet in the water. I put my arm around her, and she leaned against me while I sat and thought. I had to get Mum's address. If I could do that, then somehow I'd find a way of writing to her.

The next day, as soon as Uncle Caleb had gone to work, I went to the toilet, but on the way I dived into his study. There was a filing cabinet in the corner behind the desk. I opened the top drawer.

Letters. My heart thumped. Airmail letters. I pulled one out and nearly cried aloud with disappointment. It was some religious thing from Nelson all about how the men should demand obedience from the women. I shoved it back, eased the drawer shut again, and crept out of the room.

I sat on the toilet and thought. Mum's address had to be in there somewhere. All I had to do was find it.

The next evening, after family prayers and my fantastic singing, Uncle Caleb informed me he'd had a letter from Mum. She was well and she sent her love, and no, it was not necessary for me to read it.

I stormed out of the house without asking. Daniel and Maggie found me in the park an hour later. Maggie threw her arms around me.

"She was sure you were dead," said Daniel.

"Well, if somebody would talk to her about Miriam, then she wouldn't be worried all the time," I snapped.

He looked upset, but instead of answering, he handed me a letter. An airmail letter! In Mum's handwriting! I stared at him, my mouth open. "I collected the mail today." He often went to work with Uncle Caleb. "I did not give this to my father."

"Oh, Daniel! Thank you so much!" I let go Maggie and gave him a bear hug.

He looked a bit startled. "If my father saw you do that, then you would have to marry me!" Was he joking?

I tore the letter open, reading it greedily. Then I sat quite still, the page moving gently on my lap. It was a nothing letter. It could have been written by a fence post. She'd had a good flight. The people she was working with were very dedicated and very kind. Conditions were appalling. She was well, she hoped I was too, and she loved me always. There wasn't even an address.

"Read it." I held it out to Daniel. "It doesn't tell me anything. I still don't know why she left. Or where she is."

He took it and remarked, "My father says she repented and has seen the light."

I hugged Maggie hard. "Daniel, that's crap! Something happened. She was ordinary one day and the next day she was off to Africa. It was like she was running away."

He didn't say anything, and if he was going to keep going with the repenting bit then he could keep on saying nothing. But after a while he asked, "There was no clue at all? Nothing that was different?"

I shook my head. "No. She'd been busier than usual, but that had been going on for several months. . . ." I stopped, staring at him.

"There was something?" Daniel asked.

"The men," I whispered. "Louisa—she's our neighbor—said creepy men kept coming to visit Mum when I wasn't there."

Daniel gave me a twisted smile. "Would she think elders of the Children of the Faith were creepy?" He looked at the ground for a moment. "It could have been them. I know they travel a lot, but the children are never told why."

I put my hands over my face. Maggie threw her arms around me. "Do not cry, Esther. Please do not cry."

Daniel turned the letter over. "There is no stamp," he said. "It has been marked, but I cannot read that or the postmark." He frowned over it. "It might be a *Z* on the postmark, but the rest is too smudged to read."

"What countries start with *Z*?" I knew so little about Africa.

"Zambia or Zimbabwe." Daniel stood up, handing

the letter back to me. "Wait. She has written something here and then crossed it out."

Together, we stared at the crossed-out writing. "I can make out *sorry*," I said at last.

"And I think the rest is *I can't think why I* and that is it." Daniel looked at me. "She is sorry about something."

I felt light and almost happy. "She's sorry she ran off and left me with . . ." I stopped. I couldn't very well say "the crazy relations" in front of him.

"I have been wondering why she did," Daniel said, taking Maggie's hand and starting to walk. "It has never happened before that a dissident has repented and commended a child not brought up in the Rule to the care of the Fellowship."

"Great," I said. "I would have to be the first." And probably the last since I was determined not to be a success story from their point of view.

He smiled. "Come on. We had better get back. It will be the discipline room for you again tomorrow, I am afraid."

I groaned. "I'll leave you another message under your pillow," I promised Maggie.

We walked home, swinging her between us. Just before we got to the house, we stopped and walked like good little Pilgrims, and I put on the scarf they'd brought with them.

Daniel was right about the discipline room. I wrote Maggie her message, and drew the *O*s with their eyes shut and their mouths open in big yawns.

I had to learn Psalm 27. I learnt it in the morning, shouting out, "'When the wicked, even mine enemies and my foes, came upon me to eat up my flesh, they stumbled and fell.'"

One of the twins walked past, and I heard her giggle.

Aunt Naomi brought me my three pieces of bread at lunchtime. "The children and I are going to the Circle of Fellowship this afternoon." She put the tray down. "You would have enjoyed it, Esther. You would have been able to meet the two girls who will be going to school with you."

School! Wow and yippee! Escape.

I heard them all leave the house. They went with Uncle Caleb and Daniel after lunch. I listened until I couldn't hear the car any longer. They had to be brain-dead if they thought I'd stay in the discipline room all afternoon.

The house was quiet when I tiptoed into Uncle Caleb's study. I could hear cicadas screeching outside.

I stood for a long time, looking at the desk, the filing cabinet, and shelves. Somewhere in here there might be Mum's address. There might be the letter she had written to Uncle Caleb. I shook my head crossly. Did I want to find out, or not? I'd never get a chance like this again. I started searching. I opened the top right-hand drawer of the desk. A religious book and religious papers. The second drawer. Letters. I grabbed them, skimmed the top one.

The Fellowship wishes to commend your efforts in the great experiment. We have prayed and it has come to us that this is a godly test case, and that if it is successful then we will bend our efforts to return others to the Fellowship of the Children of the Faith. We pray for you in your travail and ask you to endure the godlessness of the child in the meantime. Know that the Fellowship remembers you and yours each day in prayer.

Now, what the hell did that mean? I looked at the date on the postmark. The day before yesterday. Were they talking about me? Was I "the child"? And if so, then what was the experiment? Return others to the Fellowship? I stared at the words, concentrating so hard that I didn't hear the sound of the car. But I did hear the footsteps. I raised my head, my breathing suspended. *No! Let me be imagining it!*

Then the door opened behind me.

Oh God, I was dead! Better for me if I was— standing there with the letter in my hand.

I couldn't move, couldn't even lift my head. I stood frozen, waiting for the words to blast me from the universe.

"Hello, Kirby."

Daniel? It was Daniel, not my uncle? And he'd called me by my own name. I collapsed into the chair. "Is Uncle Caleb here?" I whispered.

"Are you still alive?" he said, smiling and lifting his eyebrows.

I shook my head. "No, I don't think so. I think I died of fright." And what was he doing here?

"My father wanted some papers. I offered to get them for him. I thought it might be a good idea if I came instead of him." He picked up a folder from the desk.

"Thanks, Daniel. Thanks a heap."

"You are welcome," he said. "But he will probably come to check on you himself."

"Thanks. Daniel, look at this." I was still shaking as I held the letter out to him.

He didn't take it. "It is my father's letter," he said. "It is not my place to read it."

Bloody hell. "It's about an experiment," I gabbled. "About returning people to the Fellowship and enduring the godlessness of the child. Me." I took a breath. "Do you know anything about it?"

He shook his head. "No. Such matters would be decided by the Elders at their regular meetings. They might inform the adults, but the children would never be told."

"Do you think . . ."

He smiled at me. "I think I had better leave, or my father will come to find me. I know nothing about it, Kirby. I am sorry."

How could he stand it? How could he be so bloody obedient and be so happy to know nothing? I watched him drive away in a red minivan. This family seemed to have a different car every week. Would God approve? I asked myself.

I went back into the discipline room.

Twenty minutes later, Uncle Caleb showed up. He stuck his gray head around the door. "You are studying, Esther?" he asked in his gray, flat voice.

To hell and back with you. "No, Uncle Caleb. I'm missing my mother and I need to know why she left."

"It is natural and seemly for you to miss her, Esther," he said, his voice almost kind. "Keeping your thoughts with the Lord will help you."

So what did the old buzzard do? He got down on his knees and prayed. It took a thousand or so years before he left. If it hadn't been for the fact that Maggie would have been so upset, I reckon I'd have taken off right then.

Maggie was going to be upset when I did leave. But not even for Maggie could I stay here forever. I choked back a sob. At least I knew a little more now. Mum must be part of this great experiment. They wanted her back and they'd visited her and visited her and she hadn't told me.

Oh Mum, what have they done to you? And to me. A godless child to be endured.

4

A COUPLE OF WEEKS DRAGGED
past. Mum didn't write, my uncle still wouldn't give
me her address, and my life was bounded by
prayers, singing, housework, and rules. The rules
drove me wild. They were all written out and hung
on a scroll sort of thing in our bedroom. Aunt
Naomi often sent me off to read it. "Rule Ten," she
would snap. "Go and read it."

Then I'd have to recite it to her when I came
back. "A daughter respects her elders. She is modest.
She does not draw attention to herself."

"Did that not mean anything to you?" she
would sigh. "Braid your hair tidily, Esther. And do

not try to look at your reflection in the pot lids."

If you had a mirror in the house, I wouldn't have to.

But I kept on trying to find something that would show me my reflection. I had nightmares about looking in a mirror and having no face.

I didn't get to go to any Circle of Fellowship meetings. Maggie was sick, and I offered to stay with her. That earned me a smile from my aunt. When the next meeting came around, I was back in the discipline room because I totally refused to start embroidering a Bible verse like the ones the twins were doing. Aunt Naomi had caught me running down the street with the little ones. "Esther, you will begin sewing your text this evening. Here is the verse I have chosen for you."

She flipped open her Bible and pointed. "'Charity doth not behave itself unseemly, seeketh not her own, is not easily provoked, thinketh no evil.'"

"I am not sewing that," I said, through clenched teeth.

I guess it was lucky for me she decided not to make a fight out of it. Instead, she snapped, "Very well. Then you will go to the discipline room tomorrow and commit the chapter to memory."

It was the worst day I'd spent in there. There was

too much time to worry about Mum. I found it hard to breathe in that little room, and I longed for windows so I could search for my reflection.

They took me to buy my uniform on a Thursday. Aunt Naomi told me we'd all be going into town for the day. "Even Uncle Caleb?" I asked.

"All of us," she nodded, smiling. "Now go and wake the children, Esther."

Abraham and Luke were already awake and playing some game. "Time to get dressed," I said and went to get the girls up.

"Today is our town day!" Rachel sprang up and reached for her clothes.

"Yeah, well count me out," I said, handing Maggie her blouse.

"But you have to come," Rebecca said. "We all go. All of us, always."

"Look, Bex-baby—there is no way I'm going to walk into town dressed like this." There was no way I'd go anywhere I didn't have to with her parents, either, but I didn't tell her that.

They all stopped what they were doing and stared at me. "You must call me Rebecca," she said at last.

Rachel said, "You will have to come, Esther.

If you refuse, then Father will make us all pray for you."

I grabbed Maggie's pillow and thumped the wall with it. God, I just love this discipline system. Do something wrong and the whole family gets punished. "Too bad," I said, swapping the pillow for the hairbrush. "You can all suffer for ten minutes on your knees and then you can toddle off to town without me." I brushed out Maggie's hair.

"You do not understand," Rebecca said, her voice urgent. "If you refuse to go, we will all have to pray about it until you agree to go. And then you will have to spend tomorrow in the discipline room."

I said nothing, and they all stopped what they were doing and stared at me, Maggie looking like she was having trouble breathing.

Bloody, bloody hell. "All right! I'll come. It'll kill me, but I'll come."

All nine of us climbed into the big brown van Uncle Caleb had arrived home in the night before.

"How many cars has this family got?" I asked Daniel in the most accusing sort of voice I could dredge up.

He smiled—Daniel never laughed—and said, "My father owns a car-rental business. We do not have a car of our own, we just use one of the business cars." All my arguments about living modestly while you owned a dozen cars went flat.

"Aunt Naomi never drives," I said.

"She cannot. The women never do. It is a man's job."

This family! This faith! Trust the men to grab the fun jobs.

All the way into town I stared out the window, biting my lips, determined not to cry, especially not in front of them. We got out of the van. If I live a million years, nothing, but nothing, will ever be as embarrassing as walking through town with the whole bloody family and all of us wearing clothes from a hundred years ago.

If I met anyone I knew, I'd die. No, I wouldn't. I'd rush up to them and beg them to take me home with them. People looked at us. Some laughed, some smiled. A few looked pitying. I wanted to shrivel up and turn into a blob on the footpath.

We marched into a shoe shop. They bought black lace-up shoes for all the kids, starting at Daniel and going all the way down to Maggie. The only thing that surprised me was they didn't buy them for the baby that hadn't been born yet.

I saw Maggie gazing longingly at a pretty pair of blue sandals that had little red squirrels painted on them. "Uncle Caleb," I said, trying for a low and godly voice, "could Magdalene try on those sandals? They would be most suitable for this weather."

In his gray voice he answered, "Esther, you are still ignorant of the Rule or you would not suggest such infamy. We wear plain clothes. We do not decorate ourselves, for that is frivolous and unseemly and directs our thoughts away from the Lord."

So we all got plain, black, heavy, hot, lace-up shoes. Apparently the school I was going to had black lace-ups as part of the uniform. "But there must be a summer uniform," I protested.

"Sandals do not cover your feet decently," Uncle Caleb said. "You will wear shoes."

And if I could kick you with them, I would.

Next, we went to some big department store and bought the boys more horrible gray trousers and horrible gray shirts and horrible kneesocks. Gray, of course. Poor little Maggie stared around her at dresses on racks. They were actually really gross—all frills and nylon lace and shiny buttons—but her soul was in her eyes. She was dying from grayness.

The twins didn't need new uniforms, because

they were in their second year at some intermediate school. While my uncle and aunt were busy with the boys, Rachel and Rebecca managed to survey the entire floor of the shop. "I have chosen the denim shorts and the bright-pink halter top," Rachel hissed.

Rebecca waited until Uncle Caleb had gone with the boys into the fitting room, and Aunt Naomi had taken Maggie to get some plain white socks. "I will have the short purple skirt and the white T-shirt with the space cadet on the front," she whispered back. They giggled.

"We do this every year," Rachel murmured to me.

"Then when it gets boring in church, we can imagine what would happen if we actually wore such clothes," Rebecca said quickly, watching for the fitting-room door to open.

"Would you like to?" I asked.

They looked surprised. Rachel glanced over her shoulder to where Aunt Naomi was starting back toward us. "Of course not. It would not be seemly."

Rebecca shook her head. "It would grieve our parents."

Aunt Naomi was carrying a pale-blue knit shirt and a tartan kilt skirt. "This is your uniform, Esther. Please try it on."

The skirt came halfway between ankle and knee.

"Hmm," said Aunt Naomi when I waded out of the dressing room to show her, "it is a little short."

"Short?" I squeaked. "You've got to be joking!"

Uncle Caleb said, "The women of our faith always dress with modesty."

"Not at school!" I gasped. "Please!"

Aunt Naomi tweaked the waistband. "This will have to do. The next size would be much too big. Perhaps I can let the hem down." She examined it. "Not enough fabric available there, I am afraid."

I shut my eyes. I was going to die of embarrassment turning up at school like this. Only geeky dorks wore their skirts down around their shins. Rebecca came with me into the fitting room. "Do not worry," she whispered. "You just roll it over at the waist on the way to school. See?" She flicked her own waistband so neatly, she must've done it hundreds of times. "Most of the girls do it."

"Thanks!" I whispered back. I'd not paid much attention to the twins before today. They were always there and always being good. Today had surprised me more than just a bit. Rebecca just grinned, took the uniform, and left me to get back into my "seemly" clothes.

Daniel didn't get any clothes. "Your uniform still fit you?" I asked.

Sadness crossed his face, but he said calmly, "My father feels I have had sufficient schooling. I am to work with him now."

Poor Daniel. Why did he stay? I wouldn't, if I was him. Except that I was staying. Should I just walk out? And if I did, where would I go? How would I find Mum again? The old questions kept revolving in my head.

We went to the lake for lunch. "We do it every year," Rachel said. "We buy school shoes and any uniforms, then we go and have lunch at the lake."

"Always on the Thursday before school starts," Rebecca added.

We got into the van and trundled off to the lake. It'd be nice to have some café food again. I'd get a hamburger and chips.

Dreamer! We got to the lake, and it was pretty, with trees and ducks and swans and a statue of a little boy. Aunt Naomi lifted a big picnic basket out of the minibus, and the twins grabbed rugs and cushions. I took Maggie's hand, and we all marched solemnly to a wooden picnic table.

I waited for Luke and Abraham to race around

the way they did when I took them to the park, but they stood quietly while their mother put the basket down. "May we have the bread for the ducks, please?" Abraham asked.

She gave them a paper bag, and they walked down to the edge of the water.

No wonder they liked me taking them to the park.

We ate our lunch, and people walked past and stared at us. Luke, Abraham, and Maggie kept glancing longingly at the play area. The twins' eyes followed a dog chasing a Frisbee. Daniel kept his eyes on Maggie and Luke, quietly helping them so they wouldn't get prayed over. My uncle sat at the end of the table and waited while Aunt Naomi made him a sandwich.

Then he said grace, a short one today, thank goodness, but I knew we'd have an extra-long one at dinner to make up for it.

We ate lunch. I'd end up with an ulcer at this rate. Isn't it bad for you to eat while you're raging mad?

We finished eating and packed up the picnic. Uncle Caleb led the way back to the van. I saw the girl first, I think, although it's hard to be sure. She was a bit older than me, and she was standing a little above us on the slope, staring intently. Her arms were out from her sides as if she was reaching out toward us. She had long hair, the golden blond color of the twins'.

I stopped. She looked exactly like an older version of the twins.

Maggie tugged at my hand, then followed my glance. She stood dead still and her face went as white as the swans on the lake. "Miriam!" she screamed, and her voice sent shivers right through me. "It is Miriam! It is Miriam's ghost!" She buried her head in my skirt, terrified.

My own heart was doing a tap dance. But that girl was no ghost. She was flesh and blood, and her clothes were real—a skirt, longer than the one I wore, but light and patterned, and a ribbed top. "Are you Miriam?" I whispered.

She nodded, staring at Maggie, desperate to comfort her. But Uncle Caleb said sharply, "Hurry along, Esther. Put Magdalene in the vehicle, if you please."

He looked at the girl. At Miriam. His daughter. His eyes swept right over her as if she didn't exist. She cringed and bit her bottom lip, but she didn't say anything. Years of training. Years of the discipline room. Daniel hustled the boys into the van. His face was strained.

Aunt Naomi didn't even glance at her daughter. She tapped Rebecca on the shoulder. "Eyes ahead of you, please, miss."

Rachel dropped the rug she was carrying. She picked it up, managing to look at Miriam as she did. Uncle Caleb said, "We will pray for you when we reach home, Rachel." My head was whirling. I knelt and put my arms tight around Maggie. She nearly strangled me, all the time howling hysterically. Miriam took a step toward us. Uncle Caleb left the minibus and walked toward us too. She whirled around and ran back up the slope. "Tell her I'm not dead. Tell her I love her!" the girl cried. She was gone by the time Uncle Caleb reached us. I heard her crying, and Uncle bloody Caleb would have heard her, too.

"The vehicle, Esther. At once."

I got to my feet, treading on my skirt, stumbling along, carrying Maggie, thoughts jolting about in my head. If Miriam wasn't dead, then what had happened? Why had they told Maggie she was? Why wouldn't they even look at her? Did the little boys think she was dead? When she was looking at them all, her face . . . it hurt to remember. How could they do that to their own daughter? How could they see her looking like that and not make a move to go to her? To comfort her?

I stepped up into the van, put Maggie on a seat, and turned to shut the door. Miriam watched us. Watched me. I was crying, my tears making her blurry, so I couldn't see the lost look in her eyes anymore. It hurt too much. It reminded me of Mum leaving me. Walking away, and there was nothing I could do to stop her.

Nobody said anything all the way home. The only sound was Maggie's high, keening wail. I held her tight, and inside I ached for me and for her and for Miriam.

Uncle Caleb drew up in the driveway. "Help your mother unpack, then you will come to the study for prayer." He got out and strode off into the house.

I slid to the edge of the seat, trying to get down without falling over my stupid skirt and dropping Maggie. Daniel took my hand to help me. I wouldn't look at him because he'd see I'd been crying, but also because I hated him. He'd let them do this to his sister. Sisters.

"I will ask my father if you can put Magdalene to

bed instead of taking her to prayers," he said.

"Thanks," I muttered. It wasn't fair to blame him. He had no more power than I did. I don't know what he said to his father, but Uncle Caleb actually came out of the study and came over to where I was sitting in the family room, holding Maggie.

"Magdalene, listen to me if you please."

Normally, she would have shut up for a week when he used that voice on her. All she did now was rock against me and cry in that high, eerie voice, "Miriam is dead and I saw her! She is a ghost!"

He stood in front of her and addressed her as if she was an assembly. "Your sister has not died. She is dead to us because she refuses to live according to the true principles of godly life. She refuses to keep the Rule. She has damned herself forever, and her behavior would have contaminated you and her brothers and sisters."

As if Maggie would understand all that even if she could listen. But the message was probably for me rather than her.

"What did she do?" I whispered.

His gray stare shifted briefly to me before it hit the wall somewhere over my shoulder. A look of pain skidded across his face, but I didn't feel a shred of pity. "She wanted to study art. She promised she would use her talent to glorify the Lord. I spoke on her behalf to the Elders to ask permission. Art is not a subject we normally allow." He stopped and the pain set his face in concrete.

I whispered, "What happened?"

Another dose of the gray glance and I thought he wouldn't tell me, but at last he said, "She betrayed us. She was not illustrating the word of the Lord as she had promised. She painted people, contaminated people who showed their bare limbs. Male and female."

I hugged Maggie tight. "But she is your daughter!" This family was so good at ditching their daughters.

"She is dead to us. The work of her hands would contaminate our family and spread contagion to the community. We prayed that she would return to the path of righteousness, but she refused." So that was why Maggie'd had fifty fits when I said I'd draw her a picture. Uncle Caleb looked briefly in my direction and added, "She left us, Esther. We did not cast her out. But now she is dead to us unless she repents."

"How do you know she hasn't repented?"

Miriam's anguished face would stay, a picture in my head, forever.

"She was dressed like a whore," he said calmly.

"But her skirt was right down to her ankles!" I gasped.

"Her hair was uncovered, unbraided, and she had cut it."

"It was still long!"

He explained patiently and inflexibly, "The women of our faith never cut their hair. They wear it long and in a single braid. That way it does not tempt the eyes of their men to stray."

Men. Always it was the men who controlled what the women could do. But he hadn't finished. "She wore no head covering, the flesh on her arms was exposed, and her skirt was bright and gaudily patterned."

All at once, I was sick to my stomach. How could he look at his daughter and see only her clothes? How hadn't he seen the hurt and the longing? I got up. "May I put Magdalene to bed, please?"

He looked her over, as if she was a prize exhibit in a show, before he nodded. "Very well. You are both excused."

Great. Let me remember to thank you one day.

I carried Maggie into the bedroom. I kicked the pile of cushions and plopped down on them. I talked to Maggie, tried to make her listen. Clowned around and tried to make her laugh. But all she did was cry that Miriam was a dead ghost and the devil had got her.

I was frightened. She couldn't hear me, and I was sure she didn't know who I was or even where she was. I lay her on the cushions and she just grabbed hold of one and rocked backward and forward, crying.

I ran. Knocked on the study door. Burst in. "Aunt Naomi . . . can you come? Please! I don't know what to do."

Wonder of wonders, when she looked at Uncle Caleb for permission, he actually nodded. She stood up, one hand pressed into her lower back, and came with me to our bedroom. Maggie lay exactly as I'd left her, face pressed into the cushion that muffled her wailing.

Aunt Naomi marched over to her, sat beside her. Grabbed her by the shoulders and wrenched her upright. Then she pulled back her arm and slapped Maggie hard on both cheeks.

Maggie gasped, but her eyes lost the blankness, and

she stopped crying. Her mouth open, she stared at her mother as her eyes swam back into focus. Aunt Naomi took a hanky from her apron pocket and wiped Maggie's face. "That is better." She gave her a quick hug. "Now, let Esther help you get your clothes off and you can have a little rest. It has been a big day."

Maggie breathed in deeply, with only a few hiccups on the way. "Mother . . . I saw Miriam. She was a ghost."

Aunt Naomi reached for Maggie's hands and held them firmly. "No, she was not a ghost. She does not want to live a godly life anymore and that is why she left. She is dead to us, Magdalene. Do you understand?"

Maggie said nothing, her eyes huge in her blotchy face.

Aunt Naomi got up. "We will not speak of her again. Go to sleep, now."

I undressed Maggie. Usually she insisted on doing everything herself, even untying the wretched tapes on her skirt. Today she sat like a limp rag doll. I picked her up and dumped her on her bed. "Miriam gave me a message for you," I whispered. She turned her head and looked at me. "She said: 'Tell her I miss her. Tell her I love her.'"

"Why did she go away, then?" Maggie demanded, her voice wavering. "I hate her! She is mean and horrible."

She curled up in a ball, facing away from me. I rubbed her back. "And you want her back. Just like I want my mother back."

She twitched her shoulders but didn't say anything. I kept on rubbing her back and shoulders and between one second and the next she went to sleep.

I sat there, waiting until I heard them leave the study. When I went back to the family room, Aunt Naomi asked, "Is she asleep?"

I nearly yelled, *A fat lot you care!* It was only the thought of the discipline room that kept me quiet. Instead I nodded my head.

Nobody said anything. Not about the shopping, the picnic, and definitely not about Miriam. But she was there in all their thoughts.

That evening, after prayers and stuff, the twins sewed their verses with their mouths clamped shut. Usually they chatted away about nothing. Abraham didn't "accidentally" kick a door or a chair when he was sent to bed the way he normally did. Luke stayed close to him, his eyes on the floor. Daniel had a Bible in his lap but didn't turn a page all evening. Aunt Naomi went to bed an hour earlier than usual. My uncle stayed in the study.

I put down the skirt I was hemming and went and sat on the veranda. Mum. Miriam. The experiment. So many mysteries, so much sadness.

It was a long time before I slept that night.

5

THE NEXT DAY AUNT NAOMI SHOOK me awake, saying, "I want you to come to the Circle of Fellowship today, Esther. You can meet Charity and Damaris. They will be starting school with you."

I'd been dreaming of Miriam. Just in time, I shut my mouth before telling my aunt. I yawned and rubbed my eyes, trying to stay in bed for a few extra seconds while looking like I was getting up.

"Great," I muttered. "I'm really looking forward to that."

She didn't say anything then, but I got an extra dose of chores, which was actually a lot better than being prayed over.

At eight o'clock I was told to go and wake Maggie. "Wouldn't it be better to let her sleep?" I asked.

"Do not question your elders. Please go immediately." I reckon if she hadn't found me so useful, I'd have been dumped in the discipline room.

I woke Maggie. I was scared that she might be off in another world where I couldn't reach her, like yesterday. But she smiled at me. "Hello, Esther."

I hugged her. "Hello, Maggie." Should I talk to her about Miriam? Damn it, why not? I wished they'd talk to me about Mum, let me read her letter, tell me why she had left. Maggie might feel the same. Or she might have hysterics again.

I pulled her out of bed, tumbling her on the floor and tickling her. She squealed with a hand over her mouth so her father wouldn't hear. "Do you remember about yesterday?" I asked, picking her up and sitting her at the dressing table so I could brush her hair.

She sat very still. "Miriam," she whispered. "I saw Miriam's ghost."

I hugged her tight. "You thought it was her ghost because you thought—and so did I—that she was dead. But she isn't, Maggie. She just had to leave.

100

And she loves you. Remember? She said to tell you."

She twisted in the chair and stared up at me, frowning. Finally she said, "I do not like God if He does not like Miriam painting."

Oh, sweetheart, I couldn't agree more! "For chrissakes, don't let your mother or father hear you say that," I whispered.

But she was okay for the rest of the day. Not brilliant, but okay. We trundled off after lunch to the Circle of Fellowship. It was in the next street, so we could walk. Abraham stared at the low stone wall he always walked along when we went to the park, but today he kept to the footpath.

The Circle of Fellowship was the pits. Aunt Naomi introduced me to the five women, starting with the one whose place we were at. "Sister Dorcas, this is Esther."

I muttered something and stared at her. She was older than Aunt Naomi and had a well-worn look about her. Dorcas. I was quite pleased they hadn't called me Dorcas.

Then there was Leah, who turned out to be a bossy cow; and Dinah, who had the most gorgeous-looking kids, including Damaris, who was the most gorgeous of all. Charity's mother was called Hope, and she had a baby, and then there was Thomasina, who was very young and very pregnant. They called each other "Sister," and us kids called them "Aunt."

First we prayed. Then the six women took it in turns to read the Bible and talk about it. A girl a bit older than me with buck teeth and pretty, dark hair said, "I would like to read the word of the Lord, too, if you please, Aunt Dorcas."

Dorcas smiled and said, "Praise the Lord! Of course you may, Beulah."

Beulah! And buck teeth. And she was the bossy cow's daughter.

The kids sat still, and the room got hotter and hotter. Each of those women, except Thomasina, must've had around four or five kids with them.

After a million years, Dorcas said, "You older girls can take the young ones outside."

We filed out, the girls automatically reaching for their head scarves. Beulah stayed where she was. There were trees in the back garden, and the younger kids raced for them and scrambled up into the branches. That was when I had a most riveting conversation with Damaris and Charity, the two girls who'd be going to school with me.

"I suppose you will take Miriam's place now

that she is dead," said Charity, flopping down in the shade of an apple tree and whipping her scarf off.

"She's not dead," I snapped. "I saw her yesterday."

"She has broken the Rule," Damaris said. Her scarf was off as well. "My father told us that Uncle Caleb said he would pardon her and receive her back into the bosom of the family if she repented." She flicked the scarf at a fly.

That was news to me. "What good is that, if he isn't going to let her paint?" I demanded. It was so good to talk about this with people who'd talk back. But I bet they weren't supposed to be talking about it.

"She should not want to paint," Damaris said. "The word of the Lord and the Rule should be enough for her."

"Why? Why should it be enough? And where the hell does it say in the Bible that she can't paint?" I thought I'd shock them, but they both giggled.

"How many psalms do you know off by heart?" Charity asked, grinning.

"Only three, plus chapter 13 of 1 Corinthians," I said, smiling back in spite of myself.

Damaris sighed. "You would probably know the entire Bible by now if you lived in our house. My father said he thought Uncle Caleb was being too lenient and that if any of us transgressed like Miriam did, then he would cast us out before we had the chance to run away."

"Your old man's stricter than Uncle Caleb?" I asked. "Nobody could be!" I stared at her, awed. How did she manage to stay sane? She was so pretty. Real model material, with huge eyes and high cheekbones. I'd give a lot to look like that.

"Her grandfather is our leader," Charity said. "And when he is called to the Lord, then her father will take his place."

"How do you stand it?" I asked, staring at Damaris.

"I like it," she said. "I like to keep the Rule. I feel safe in the love of the Lord. My faith means a lot to me."

I was shocked. Really shocked. How could a kid my age want to live the way they did? I turned to Charity. She laughed at me. "Yes, me too!" she said. "There is so much hate and unhappiness in the world. But not in our families."

"Try mine," I muttered.

Their faces grew serious. "I think Miriam was wicked," Damaris said at last. "She has brought great unhappiness to her family and to the whole community."

"She's unhappy too!" I burst out. "You didn't see her! She's aching to come home."

"It is easy then," said Charity. "She can just come back. We think Uncle Caleb is amazingly kind to her."

"For crying down the sink!" I yelled. "Is it kind to stop somebody using their God-given talent?"

"She must find some other way of channeling that talent so that it is in tune with God's law," Damaris said.

"Like what?" I snapped.

"Needlework, gardening. Creating a beautiful garden is glorifying the Lord. Producing children and nurturing them in God's love."

"Or she could have done what she promised she would do and illustrate the word of the Lord."

Shit.

Damaris slid a look at me. "Which brings us back to the original question: are you going to take Miriam's place?"

"I guess I do already." I lay on my back and pulled my stupid skirt up to sun my legs. "I get to do heaps of housework and baby-sitting."

"No," said Charity, "we do not mean like that."

"Well, what do you mean, then?"

"Miriam's chosen partner was Gideon," said

Damaris, and then she shut up. There was an electric silence.

"What d'you mean, her 'chosen partner'?"

Damaris was staring at me. "The man she was to marry."

"On her sixteenth birthday," Charity added.

They had my attention. I sat up in a hurry. "You're kidding!"

"We had the betrothal celebration on her fourteenth birthday," said Damaris. "It was fun."

I couldn't take it in. Sixteen? Married? I stared from one to the other of them, sitting there in the sun in an ordinary New Zealand back garden in the twenty-first century.

"Did she like him?" I managed to ask at last.

"Oh, yes. He is nice. We all like Gideon. He is fun—not intense, like Daniel." Damaris pulled a face.

Charity giggled. "Damaris is to be betrothed to Daniel, but she is not very happy about it. That is why she hopes you will not take Miriam's place."

Damaris smiled dreamily. "I would much rather have Gideon. I like him so much—and he will be twenty when I am sixteen."

I couldn't say anything, my jaw wouldn't work. I

just stared at them and felt very pale and very shaky. "Do you think," I asked slowly, struggling to form each word, "do you really think that Uncle Caleb will try to marry me off? At sixteen?"

"Why would you not want to be married?" Charity asked. "It is what all girls of our faith want."

May the good Lord save me! I shut my eyes. "How many are there in your faith?" I asked. How many men did they have who wanted wives, and was that why they were so all-fired keen to get Mum back? A marriageable woman with a marriageable daughter.

"There are twenty-three families in Wanganui," Damaris said. "But we might all move to Nelson and join a community there. They were talking of it before Miriam died. . . ."

"She isn't dead!" I said through gritted teeth, but they just smiled at me and carried on as if I hadn't spoken.

"My father says it will be easier to keep the Rule if the children are not exposed to evil influences while they are growing up," Charity said.

Didn't their mothers have any opinions? "When d'you think they'll go?" I'd be out of it by then, for sure.

Damaris flipped over on her stomach. "Soon, my father thinks. We will have our own school, too. It will be so much better."

I shivered in the hot sun and looked into a future where there would be nobody who thought the same way I did. A future that was going to be increasingly difficult to escape from.

Damaris was watching me. "If you do not like it, why do you not just walk out? That is what Miriam did."

I sat with my head leaning on my hunched-up knees. "I don't think I could. My mother . . . How would my mother find me again? I don't even have her address. And Maggie. Maggie's a mess right now. And where would I go? Where did Miriam go?"

Charity shrugged. "My father says she wandered around until the police picked her up. They took her home, and Uncle Caleb refused to have her back unless she repented, so they took her away again."

"There is a guidance counselor at our school. Go and see her on Monday," Damaris suggested. "She could tell you how to get away."

She sure was keen to get rid of me. "You don't need to worry about your precious Gideon. Nobody, but nobody, is going to tell me who to marry.

Especially not when I'm only sixteen." *Especially not to somebody who believes the dumb stuff you guys believe.*

Just then, Dorcas called us in to help prepare afternoon tea. It was pretty sumptuous; she must've been cooking all day. We called the children in. Abraham was the oldest male there, so he got to say grace. It bugged the hell out of me the way the women put themselves in the background.

The kids all waited politely while the women handed the plates around. They only took one cake or sausage roll at a time. They didn't talk with a full mouth. They didn't fight or push or spill their drinks. It made me sick.

"Did you have a nice chat with Damaris and Charity?" Aunt Naomi asked on the way home.

"Yes," I said. "It was most enlightening."

"They are lovely girls," said my aunt sadly. Thinking of Miriam, I guess—more important in her absence than she ever was when she was with them, I'd be willing to bet.

On Sunday we went to church as usual, but what was different for me was that I started looking at people instead of keeping my head down, swearing to myself and wishing I was back home. As we were having the fellowship meal afterward, Charity and Damaris grabbed me. "Aunt Naomi, may Esther help us pour the tea?"

Aunt Naomi smiled, "Of course. I am happy to see her fitting in."

Maggie hadn't let go of my skirt all morning, so we took her with us. Charity pulled up a chair. "You pour the milk, Magdalene."

It was a great job for finding out who people were. All the adults were called "Aunt" and "Uncle." "Are you all related?" I asked.

Damaris giggled. "Heavens no! Only by faith."

I poured tea for Aunt Adah—not a name I'd keep in my head in case I ever did have children—and one for Uncle Theophilus. Holy hell! Not that he came and got it himself. His daughter, who was called Kezia, trotted over and got it for him. "Gideon was asking where you were," she hissed at Damaris.

"Really?" Damaris's face glowed.

Kezia was busting with news. "And Daniel heard him!"

So what? That was significant? It seemed that it was.

"What did he say?" Charity gasped.

Kezia glanced at Maggie, but she was carefully

wiping up three drops of spilled milk. "Nothing! Absolutely nothing. I swear to you!"

Charity and Damaris absorbed this stunning piece of news. It seemed to me that it swelled inside them until they were about to burst with the impact of it.

"So what?" I cried at last. "What's so G—er—really important about him saying nothing?"

They looked at me, pity in their eyes. "He is intended for Damaris. If he wants to keep her"—and Charity's tone suggested, Who *wouldn't* want to keep her—"then he should be making it clear that she is his."

I poured tea for the very young, very pregnant woman who had been at the Circle of Fellowship, Aunt Thomasina. She took it and one for her husband, who sat on his chuff and let that poor girl run after him. His hands were too big for his wrists, his hair was spiky and stuck out from his head, and she smiled at him like he was God on earth.

I turned back to the other three girls. "So how does he make it clear that Damaris is his?" In my world, he'd put his arm around her and kiss her and stare into her eyes, but I couldn't see that happening here.

Kezia was scornful. "You do not know much, do you? He should have said to Gideon, 'She is over there, would you like me to pass on your good wishes?'"

"Or he could have said," Charity added, "something like, 'She is doing what she does every Sunday, and do you not think the light of the Lord is in her face this day?'"

"Is that instead of saying she's looking particularly gorgeous today?" I asked.

They giggled. "Oh, we would never say that! That is vanity!"

So that was why they had no mirrors.

Damaris pushed the cups at Kezia. "You had better go. Aunt Adah is frowning."

Kezia took the cups and went. Damaris stared after her, then she gave a little skip. "Oh, I hope . . ." Her face fell. "It is uncharitable to have such thoughts when it has all come about from such unhappiness." She gently touched Maggie's cheek.

I poured more tea, my head in a whirl. They were good, these girls. Good and kind, and they liked their narrow, weird lives. Why did I feel bad? Why did I feel as if it was all choking me—the clothes, the ideas, the people? I'd been so sure I was right and they were wrong. Now it was starting to feel as if it was just me who was wrong.

Tomorrow there was school and ordinary people and guidance counselors. And mirrors. I couldn't wait.

We drove home from church in a car called a Chariot. It was green and had a dent in the front door. Daniel drove, saying nothing. The twins chattered away and Abraham and Luke threw a ball of paper backward and forward, carefully, so their parents wouldn't notice. Maggie leaned against me and sucked her thumb.

"My mother looks tired," Daniel said to his father. "Would you like me to take the children to the beach this afternoon?"

There was a gasp as five sets of eyes swung around and riveted themselves on Uncle Caleb. He looked at Aunt Naomi and, Daniel was right, she looked exhausted for once. After an age, Uncle Caleb nodded, "Very well. You are responsible for upholding the Rule, Daniel."

We raced into the house to collect towels. "Are we allowed to swim?" I asked Rachel.

She shook her head. "But we can paddle. And somebody always falls in!" She giggled.

Daniel got the garden spades and a couple of buckets, and we were off. The journey was very different from the one home from church. The kids bounced and sang and laughed. Daniel made no attempt to "discipline" them. We got to the beach, and they tumbled out. He did set some limits then. "Do not go where you cannot look back and see me. Stay on the beach. Try not to get your clothes wet."

The kids were off, running barefoot over the sand, splashing into the waves.

"Will it be the discipline room for you if they all come back soaked?" I asked.

He smiled suddenly—if Damaris could see him now, she'd change her mind about not wanting to marry him. "I do not know, but I will surely find out!"

"Damaris thinks you don't want to marry her."

He sighed and stretched himself out in the sun, pulling up his trouser legs and rolling up his shirtsleeves. I sat down too, hoping he'd talk about it, because I was bursting with curiosity. "She is right," he said softly, as if to himself.

"She's very pretty and very nice," I offered, hoping he'd keep going.

"And she keeps the faith and lives by the Rule.

She will make an excellent wife." He sounded about as enthusiastic as a dead fish.

"So why don't you want to marry her?" A thought struck me—he could be gay.

Silence, then he whispered, "I do not want to marry Damaris, or anybody." He *was* gay? "I want to go to university. I want to be a doctor."

I was staring at him. "What are you going to do?"

His hands were busy shredding a piece of dry seaweed. "I cannot do anything. I go every day to work with my father. My life is planned for me."

"But you aren't going to marry Damaris," I said. "So does that mean . . . ?" I couldn't finish.

He hunched up his shoulders. "I do not know what it means. Not yet. I just do not know."

We said nothing more, but watched the twins swing Maggie up over a wave—and all three of them ended up with their skirts wet even though they were tucked into their gross underwear. Daniel straightened and threw his shirt around his pale shoulders. "I really wanted to come here because I have something to tell you," he said. "It is difficult to talk to you at home."

"Have you got another letter from Mum?" I asked, my heart accelerating.

He shook his head. "My father had one on Tuesday." I gasped, furious, but Daniel went on, "I asked him if I could read it and he gave it to me. It was not really any different from the one you had. She said, 'Thank you for caring for my daughter, my heart and loving thoughts are with her always.'"

I dug my hands into the hot sand, scrunched up handfuls and screwed them so tight the sand was forced out of my fists. "Why? Why did she do it?"

He drew in the sand. "I do not know. But I looked through her luggage for you."

My head flicked around, all hint of tears vanishing. "Daniel! Oh, thank you! Did you find anything?"

He shook his head. "Not really. Only this." He pulled an envelope out of his pocket and tipped it up into his hand. Tiny pieces of paper fell out.

I stared at them. "What . . . ?"

"This was wrapped in a T-shirt."

"Which one?" I asked sharply. It seemed to me, sitting there on the beach, that the T-shirt was important. Which just shows how desperate and crazy I was getting.

"It was pink and it had stains on one shoulder."

"Oh!" A sob choked out of me. Her slob-around-home T-shirt. A picture flashed into my head. "She was wearing it the day the letter came that told her she could go to Africa." I stirred the tiny balls of paper.

Daniel picked up one of the pieces. "I tried to read it, but the pieces are too small. It cannot have been about Africa. Why would she tear up a letter like that? Why would she keep the pieces? I do not think this was an ordinary letter." He threw a piece of seaweed so that it went skittering over the sand.

I screwed up my eyes, trying to remember. "She went really pale," I said, "and she screwed the letter up and shoved it in her pocket." I swallowed a lump in my throat. "After that, I couldn't talk to her. She was just . . ." I couldn't go on.

Daniel touched my hand. "I wish I knew more. I wish I could help you. Who would write to your mother? What could they write about that might upset her so badly she had to run away? And are they still trying to get in touch with her? It must be tied up with the experiment. That is what I do not like about the Rule. I hate not understanding things. I hate not knowing things that are there to know." The words burst out of him, a dam where the spillway had suddenly opened.

"Daniel . . . I'm sorry. I'm so sorry." I held on to his hand, feeling as if I was out swimming in the waves, and they were way over my head.

He turned and gave me a funny, twisted smile. "If I had told this to Damaris, she would have been shocked and upset. She would have prayed for me." He looked at our two hands. "I cannot marry Damaris, Kirby."

It felt strange to hear my own name again. "What else can't you do, Daniel?" I asked quietly in case somehow the breeze picked the words up and carried them to Uncle Caleb.

"I do not know yet. I just do not know." He took a deep breath and let go my hand. "That is my problem. Shall we talk about yours?" He smiled again. "Yours is much easier."

I screwed up my face. "I'm glad you think so."

"I think you had better go and talk to Mrs. Fletcher at school. She is the guidance counselor. I think you had better tell her everything you know about your mother. She might be able to suggest a reason why she ran away."

Excitement ran through me. Fast following it came another thought. "Uncle Caleb would kill me."

"Yes," Daniel agreed. "We are not permitted to

speak to teachers except to answer questions in class."

"And you are telling me to do this? You are telling me to break the Rule?" I asked.

"Yes," he whispered. "I am."

Oh, Daniel! It will be worse for you than for me.

All five of the children were soaked to the skin by the time we had to go home. "We will do the washing," the twins said, glancing anxiously at Daniel. "Mother will not have to do it."

"That is kind." He smiled at them. "Did you enjoy yourselves?"

"Yes!" from every kid. Funny—an afternoon at the beach and they weren't allowed to swim or take off their heavy clothes and they'd had a ball. If you don't have much, little things are really special. There must be a moral in that somewhere.

Uncle Caleb didn't go ballistic when we turned up with our dripping cargo. He was concerned about Aunt Naomi. Adah was there, and my aunt was in bed. The kids tiptoed around. Obviously this didn't happen often either.

"Is the baby coming?" I asked Daniel.

He shook his head. "I hope not. It should not come until March."

"Will they get a doctor?"

"Yes, if she needs one. They believe in modern medicine."

Did he realize he'd said "they believe," and not "we believe"?

6

MAGGIE WOKE ME THE NEXT MORNING. "I am going to school today, Esther!"

I hugged her and wished she had something special to wear—a cute playsuit or even a pretty dress. Your first day of school is special. Not Maggie's. It was on with the heavy skirt and the long-sleeved blouse. Did she know the other kids would stare at her and think she was weird?

I braided her hair, a lighter gold than the twins'—and Miriam's. Then I got into my uniform. It was actually fun putting it on. When I realized that I seriously feared for my sanity. But to have my arms exposed and nothing swishing around my ankles was heaven.

Aunt Naomi was staying in bed for the day, but she called me in. "Let me braid your hair, Esther. You must keep to the Rule while you are at school. It is very important. Do you understand?"

"Yes, Aunt Naomi." Ouch! She attacked my hair as if the devil himself had to be got out of it. "Who is taking Magdalene to school, Aunt?"

She patted my head. "There! That is as seemly as I can make your hair. Do not forget your scarf. Daniel will take Magdalene to school, but I would like you to collect her and the boys afterward."

"Yes, Aunt."

Damaris and Charity came for me, and the three of us walked to the bus stop together. As soon as we got there, they flipped their waistbands over to shorten their skirts. They helped me. "I'd never worn a skirt before I came here," I grumbled.

"But what did you wear to school last year?" Damaris asked.

"Shorts or track pants. We could wear them, or a skirt. I'm allergic to skirts," I said gloomily. They laughed and tucked their head scarves into their bags. I shook my hair out of the plait, but they left theirs alone.

"We do just enough to stop us getting teased," said Charity.

"Don't you mind breaking the Rule?" I asked.

Damaris said, "We prayed about it and it came to us that the Lord was not offended."

Good of Him. I just managed not to say the words aloud. The first thing I did when I got to school was rush to the toilets. "Did you not go before you left home?" Damaris asked.

I grinned at her. "There are mirrors in toilets! I want to see if I'm still here."

"We will wait for you," Charity said, and she smiled at me.

It was strange, looking at myself again. I couldn't get over how I still looked the same. If I could have seen a reflection of my mind, it would have been so different, I wouldn't have been able to recognize it, but there was the outside me—same wild hair, same big brown eyes, same everything. I sighed and went back to the others.

Charity, Damaris, and I were all in the same class.

"Now, who are you?" asked my form teacher, who told us her name was Ms. Chandler.

"Kirby Greenland," I answered automatically.

She frowned. "Your name isn't on my list."

"Oh." I frowned. "Esther Pilgrim. Is that there?"

She found it. "Yes, that's here. Now, what is your name, young woman? Are you Esther, or are you Kirby?"

A good question. Who was I? I wasn't sure I knew anymore.

Charity came up and took my arm. "She is Esther Pilgrim, Ms. Chandler."

The teacher gave us both a hard stare, but she didn't say anything. I got another piercing stare when I asked her if I could see the guidance counselor, but she told me where Mrs. Fletcher's office was.

I found it after getting lost twice. "Come in," she said as I knocked. I opened the door and went in. She reminded me of Louisa—not thin, but not fat either. A cheerful face with lots of lines and smooth gray hair.

"Hello there!" She gave me a swift once-over with sharp eyes. "New uniform. You're a Year Nine. What's your name, ducky?"

Ducky! For chrissakes! "Actually," I said, "I'm a new Year Ten, and my name is Kirby Greenland. Or Esther Pilgrim. Take your pick."

Suddenly I had every atom of her attention focused on me. "You take your pick," she said, her voice friendly. "What shall I call you?"

"Kirby," I said slowly. "I'm not Esther, I'm Kirby."

"Well, that's a start. Sit down, Kirby who isn't Esther, and tell me all about it."

"It's not about that," I said, hesitating and stumbling and tripping over my words the way my feet did over my dumb skirt. "At least, it's not really. It's about . . ." and to my absolute, total horror, I burst into tears.

She handed me a box of tissues and sat there perfectly calmly while I blubbered my heart out. "Sorry!" I hiccuped. "I didn't know this was going to happen. I'm sorry."

A bell rang and I jumped. "Don't worry about that," she said. "We'd better get you sorted before you face the masses. Now, what's it all about?"

"It's my mother!" More tears. "I looked after her. Always. She couldn't even pay a bill or decide what to have for tea. I did all that. I told her when we needed to do the washing, when we needed to go shopping. I wrote the lists. And we were happy. She was always laughing. She used to hug me. We'd do crazy stuff, like walk on the beach in a storm, drive to Thames from Auckland just for a feed of fish-and-chips." I stopped and the words burst out of me. "She loved me. I know she did!"

"Loved?" said Mrs. Fletcher. "Why do you say 'loved'?"

"She went away. She went to Africa to work with refugees. And she didn't talk to me about it. She didn't even tell me till the day she went. And she left me with the crazy relations and they have turned me into Esther Pilgrim. And I don't even know Mum's address and my uncle won't tell me." I heard in my voice all the agony and all the pain that I'd heard in Daniel's voice, that I'd seen in Miriam. That I feared for Maggie. I clamped my jaw shut and dug my fingernails into my palms. I wouldn't cry anymore.

"Let the tears come," Mrs. Fletcher said, smiling at me. "It's a way for your body to release all that built-up stress."

I put down my head and howled. Eventually, I managed to tell her about the torn-up letter, about the experiment, and about Maggie and Miriam and Daniel.

"Miriam will be fine," she said. I looked astonished and she grinned. "You're not the first Pilgrim girl to weep her heart out in this office! Miriam is strong. She misses her family, but she will be fine. She's doing well."

"Where is she?" I asked.

"In Wellington now. She's gone to live with an uncle and his family. He broke away from the church years ago. It took us a while to discover if she had any other relatives, but we got there. They love her and she's settling well."

"But on Thursday . . . I saw her. She was so unhappy!"

"Yes, she told me about that. She had to come, she said. It was sort of saying good-bye. She also wanted Magdalene to know she wasn't dead." Her eyes were bright and very kind as she looked at me. "She came to see me afterward and have a little weep. She told me about you, although she didn't know who you were. 'She's kind,' she said. 'She loves my little sister.'"

"But what'll I do about Maggie?" I wailed. "I can't stay there much longer! And it'll destroy her if I 'die' too!"

She sighed. "There is no easy answer to that one, Kirby. You can't sacrifice yourself for Magdalene. You'd crack. She will certainly be hurt when you do go. Perhaps you can start preparing her now. Telling her you will leave when your mother comes back. Start training the twins to take your place."

I didn't want to do that! I'd miss Maggie always running first to me. I'd miss being the special one for her. I knew it was selfish, but it felt like she was all I had.

"Why did Mum go away like that?"

"Tell me what you know about her history," Mrs. Fletcher said.

"She never left me! Never! Even when she had to go on courses and stuff, she'd ring me up every night. That's why I can't understand! It doesn't make sense."

Mrs. Fletcher gave me another tissue. "I mean her history before you were born. What do you know about that?"

I rubbed my eyes and sniffed. "Only that she left home on her sixteenth birthday. She said she couldn't live there any longer."

"She was brought up in the faith, wasn't she?"

I nodded. "She wouldn't talk about it. That's all I know. And that her father used to belt her."

Mrs. Fletcher sat quiet, frowning, then she said, "There isn't very much to go on, I'm afraid."

I thumped the table. "I just need to know! I hate not knowing!" Me and Daniel. We both needed to know things.

"I think the best thing is for me to try to find out where she is."

"Don't talk to my uncle!"

"It's all right," she said, "I understand what would happen if I did. I worked with Miriam, remember."

"Do I have to go on living there? Can't I run away like Miriam did?"

Mrs. Fletcher sighed. "It's not straightforward. You aren't being abused physically and it would be difficult to say you were being mentally abused. If your uncle wanted you back, then the law would be on his side. Your mother has placed you in his guardianship. With Miriam it was different. She'd got to the point where she couldn't take any more. And her family refused to have her back unless she agreed to unreasonable conditions." She frowned and stared off into space, tapping the pencil on her teeth again. "I feel the easiest way around it all is for me to try to contact your mother." She snapped her gaze back to me. "Can you hang on in there for a while? It could take a day or two to find out which organization she's with, and after that it could take a while to get hold of her."

I slumped back in my chair, relief washing over

me in giddy waves. "Yes, I can wait. It was not being able to do anything, or find out anything that made it so hard."

"I know." She patted my hand. "And in the meantime, you start working on Magdalene."

I got up. "All right." I didn't want to. I still didn't want to. Maggie was the only person who loved me.

"You must!" said Mrs. Fletcher sharply.

"I will! I said I will, and I will." *But not just yet.*

"Starting from today." Mrs. Fletcher put a steely hand on my arm.

"But then nobody will love me!" I wailed, the tears running again.

"You might be able to love yourself, though," she replied. "Which is a reasonably important concept. Now, do you promise?"

"Loving is hard when you don't love yourself." Mum had said that. In the motel that awful night.

I sat down again, my butt on the very edge of the seat. I would have to. I couldn't stay in that family, not for much longer. Even the thought of going back there after the freedom of being at school for one day filled me with dread. "I promise," I muttered. Then I lifted my head. "I promise. I love Maggie. I don't want her to be hurt." I should have felt good.

Uplifted and noble. All I felt was hollow and angry.

"Very well," said Mrs. Fletcher. "I'll begin immediately on the hunt for your mother. Give me both her names, will you. We don't know which one she's using right now."

"Ellen Greenland. Martha Pilgrim." Even Mum didn't seem real anymore.

Mrs. Fletcher stood up when I did. She held out her arms. "Come here, Kirby!" She wrapped her arms around me and hugged me tight. "Now you hang in there! Things are moving! Do you understand?"

It was immensely comforting. I nodded against her shoulder and felt terribly, terribly tired. "Yes. I do. Thank you."

She let me go. "I'll let you know the second I find anything out—even if it isn't very important. Okay?"

I managed a wobbly smile. "Thanks. That'd be great."

I found my way back to my form room. Charity and Damaris had saved me a seat beside them. "You look awful!" Damaris whispered.

"I've got the world's worst headache," I muttered.

They dragged me up to Ms. Chandler. "Can we

take Esther to the nurse? She has a bad headache."

I had the feeling Ms. Chandler was a bit sorry I'd landed in her class. The look she gave me was less than friendly, but she let us go. Charity and Damaris demanded to know the whole story, but all I told them was that Mrs. Fletcher was going to try to contact Mum for me. I couldn't tell them how I'd made a right idiot of myself and bawled my eyes out. I could tell Daniel, but not them. I began to see why Daniel didn't want to marry Damaris, even though she was beautiful and kind and good.

I plaited my hair on the bus on the way home. Damaris and Charity walked with me to Maggie's school. They had to collect brothers and sisters as well. I had to look for Maggie. She was playing in the sandpit with two other little girls, and when she saw me she came racing over. "I love school, Esther! It's so much fun!"

"Say: *It is*, not *it's*," Charity said gently.

"It is so much fun!" Maggie repeated.

"I'm glad," I said, shooting a look at Charity to see if she'd correct me as well, but she didn't.

"Where are Abraham and Luke?" I asked.

"They are playing on the tower," Maggie said, pointing.

We went to get them and walked home together. I chatted to all three of them. I said I hoped the boys were looking out for Maggie at school. And my heart hurt. Maggie skipped and hopped and chattered.

At home, Aunt Naomi was sitting in the kitchen. She looked a bit better, but not much. The twins were home already and had made afternoon tea. We all sat around and talked about the day. Maggie plonked herself down on my knee. I gave her a hug, then picked her up and slid her in between the twins, who were sitting on the window seat. "Keep them in order, Maggie. I'll start dinner. My aunt looks tired."

Like I felt. The twins got up and cleared the table. "Here, Magdalene, you put the biscuits away in the tin," said Rebecca. It was easy. The twins loved her too. She was their sister, not mine.

"I will help you," Maggie said, dancing up to me after she'd finished the biscuits.

I grinned at her. "Thanks. Could you drag the twins out to the garden and get some veggie— vegetables—for dinner?"

The three of them went off happily. Aunt Naomi told the boys to clean all the shoes for tomorrow and then to work in the garden for an hour. I cut up meat for a casserole. "Are you all right, Aunt?" I asked.

"Yes, I will be, thank you, Esther. I just have to rest." Mum would have told me all the gory details about why she had to rest and what had gone wrong. Not my aunt.

"Have you thought of a name for the baby?" I asked. Anything to keep the black emptiness out of my head.

"Your uncle has decided on Bartholomew for a boy and Zillah for a girl."

On the whole, I hoped it'd be a girl. Bartholomew, unshortened—what a handle! "Do you like those names?"

"Of course. They are what my husband has chosen."

I chopped onions and cried. I wanted my own mother, who had called me Kirby because, she said, it sounded strong and modern.

Uncle Caleb and Daniel came home, and we had dinner after Uncle Caleb had said grace. We ate while the twins talked about their teachers. They were in different classes; Rebecca had a man called Mr. Fitzsimmons, and Rachel had a woman called Ms. Terry.

"You will call her Miss or Mrs.," Uncle Caleb said. "She is either married or not. I suggest you call her Miss."

"Yes, Father," said Rachel, her eyes wide.

Luke had the same teacher as last year, and Abraham had a new one. "She's cool!" he said.

Uncle Caleb skewered him with his eyes. "Do not use unseemly language, Abraham. Try again, if you please."

"Miss Rivers is a very nice person," Abraham said, screwing up his face.

Then my uncle turned his attention on me. "You wore your hair unbraided today, Esther." A statement, not a question. So how did he know? Daniel gave me a quick look, a tiny nod. Admit it?

"Yes," I said.

"At least you are honest." Thanks, Daniel! "But in future, you will keep your hair braided. The women of our faith are modest in thought and appearance. Braided hair does not draw attention to itself."

It was too much. I'd had enough of what I could and couldn't do. Mainly couldn't. "It's my hair and I'll wear it how I like!" I jumped up and glared at him. There was a sizzling silence. Nobody defied him like that, at least not until I'd arrived.

"Resume your seat, child." He put down his knife and fork and placed his palms flat on the table. All his concentration was beamed on me. I sat down, anger boiling in my blood. "That was a most unseemly display," he said. It was the way he said it that got me. It was impersonal. He wasn't even mad. "We will pray for you after the meal."

I jumped up again. "No! I won't be prayed over! I won't wear my hair in a dumb plait—it looks ghastly and I hate it! No dumb man is going to lust after my hair, it's the most stupid rule I ever heard!"

Dead, stark silence. Shocked faces. Maggie's mouth open. Daniel's face white. "Go to your room and wait until I call you for prayer," he said in that same impersonal voice. "You will spend tomorrow in the discipline room and you will braid your hair."

And not go to school? To hell and back with him! It really got to me that he didn't react. He was just giving the standard response, and there wasn't a scrap of emotion. At least, that's what I felt afterward, when I was trying to work out why I did what I did next.

I leapt up from the table—my chair went flying. I rushed to the sink, seized the big knife that I'd used to cut up the meat, and with my other hand I grabbed my hair in its godly braid. "If you think my hair is a temptation, then there's a way around that!" I hacked at the plait, sawing the knife backward and forward across my hair. Aunt Naomi kept her knives sharp, but even so, it hurt, pulling and tugging. I thought I'd cried enough that day never to cry again. I was wrong. I howled and hacked until my hair lay in my hand, still in its braid. I felt the stuff left on my head frizz out into a wild halo.

It was plain they didn't know what to do with me. None of the children moved. Aunt Naomi sat staring at her plate. It wasn't up to her to work out what to do with me. She waited calmly for Uncle Caleb to decide. "Go to your room and wait," he said at last. I noticed a slight wobble in his voice, and I was fiercely glad. I threw my hair and the knife on the floor and left.

It was a long prayer session that night. We didn't have any singing, it was all praying for me and how I had transgressed and needed to see the light and walk in the path of righteousness. Praise the Lord.

The whole damned Rule got recited with *Praise the Lord*s after each part.

I was sent to bed at the same time as Maggie. "Do not talk to your sister," Uncle Caleb ordered. So I winked at her and made shadow animals on the wall. When the twins came to bed, I whispered, "Please can you look out for Magdalene tomorrow? Give her a hug and stuff?"

They nodded. Rebecca whispered, "Your hair is a mess!"

I pulled a face. "An ungodly mess!"

All three girls giggled, their hands over their mouths. Then Rebecca stopped giggling and whispered, "Beulah would have told on you." She dropped her voice even lower. "She is a cow."

Maggie and Rachel stared at her. Such unseemly language. "Sorry!" Rebecca didn't look sorry. "But watch out for her. She is fifteen and thinks she can boss us all because she will be getting married next month."

"Poor Eli," Rachel added. "Except that he is so pathetic, he deserves her."

"I don't know her," I whispered. "So how can I watch out for her?"

"Yes, you do!" Rachel said. "She is the one at the

fellowship meeting who thought she was too old to come outside with us."

"Oh!" I did remember. "Skinny, with buck teeth and pretty hair."

"Outward appearance does not matter," Rebecca recited. "It is the purity of the soul that should concern you, child."

"The price of a good woman is above rubies," Maggie added, then asked, "What does that mean? How much was Ruby's price?"

We giggled again, heard footsteps, leapt to our respective beds, and tried to look holy and seemly and godly.

Aunt Naomi glanced around. "Good night, girls. Say your prayers and may God keep you until morning."

I had to learn two psalms the next day. Uncle Caleb came to see me before he left for work. "You will pay particular attention to verses three and four of this psalm." He jabbed a finger at them, "And to verse eleven of this one." He didn't look at me once.

I stayed in that room and hated it and Uncle Caleb and the whole world. My hair stuck out around my head, and I knew I looked a fright. Verses three and four went like this:

Who shall ascend into the hill of the Lord?
or who shall stand in his holy place?
He that hath clean hands, and a pure heart;
who hath not lifted up his soul unto vanity,
nor sworn deceitfully.

I imagined having a conversation with Uncle
Caleb along the lines of: Uncle, I find it difficult to
relate to the psalms—they are all about men. *He, his,*
him all the way, Uncle.

But I figured I was in enough trouble right now.
My eyes flicked to verse eleven:

For thy name's sake, O Lord,
pardon my iniquity; for it is great.

I had never even heard of words like *iniquity* and
transgression before I came here.

I learned the psalms, but at first I didn't have the
heart to yell and shout. I gritted my teeth. They
wouldn't grind me down. They wouldn't destroy
me. I took a deep breath and shouted, "'Let me
not be ashamed. Let not mine enemies triumph
over me.'"

All day, my fingers kept straying to my hair. I

tried to look at my reflection by running water into the basin when I went to the toilet, but it didn't work. I wished I hadn't cut it. But I was glad I'd got under Uncle Caleb's skin.

Aunt Naomi brought me my midday bread and water. She looked awful. "Aunt, I think you should lie down. I promise I will be obedient—or would you like me to prepare dinner?"

"I am well, Esther. You do not need to concern yourself and you must stay here all day."

Mum would have hugged me and said *Thanks for being so concerned* and *Yes, I'd love you to cook dinner, you're a wonderful, wonderful person, and what have I done to deserve you?*

Nobody ever said thank you for anything in this house. Except for passing the bread and stuff like that. I had never once heard Uncle Caleb or Aunt Naomi say thank you to any of us kids. Not to Daniel for always looking out for the little boys, not to the twins for doing the ironing every day, not to Luke and Abraham for working in the garden, not to Maggie for doing more around the house than most teenagers do. And definitely not to me.

I sighed and learned another verse. Wondered how Mrs. Fletcher was getting on with tracing Mum.

Wondered why Mum had run away when she was sixteen. Was it because she didn't want to marry the guy they'd chosen for her? What had she done? Where had she gone? I knew so little about her life.

The twins cooked dinner that night. I was allowed to do the dishes all by myself. Daniel asked if he could dry them, but Aunt Naomi said, "You must ask your father."

"Thanks, Daniel!" I flashed him a grateful smile. "But it's okay. Really."

He smiled back briefly, before his face resumed its normal, solemn expression.

The twins set out homework on the table and Maggie, full of importance, joined them. Abraham and Luke rushed through theirs, and when I'd finished the dishes, they were taking a plug to bits and had pieces of wire and tools all over the deck. Daniel mowed the lawn. Then we prayed and sang and I got to say my psalms. My uncle prayed some more and he demanded that vanity be expunged from my soul. Where did he learn these words?

Aunt Naomi said to me, "Take these with you into the discipline room, Esther. You may work on them, seeing you have memorized the psalms."

She handed me a couple of squares of heavy,

white material. "What are they?" Certainly not handkerchiefs.

"Table napkins for Beulah." Rebecca pulled a face. "You have to hem them with a herringbone stitch."

Oh, what fun! "What is a herringbone stitch, Aunt?"

She gave me one of those didn't-your-mother-ever-teach-you-anything looks and showed me how to do it. I'd rather learn psalms.

Then I had a brilliant idea. I hemmed away industriously, but I didn't tie knots in the ends of the cotton. When dear Beulah washed my table napkins, they'd unravel. Just like my hair.

I felt like a freak going to school the next day. Charity and Damaris gasped and giggled. "I will straighten it, if you like," Charity offered. "I have some scissors."

"Thanks," I said gratefully. "It must look ghastly."

"It would not be so bad if it was not a lot longer on one side," said Damaris. "What happened?"

I told them while Charity snipped. They were shocked, I know they were. But Charity only said, "I have always wanted to cut somebody's hair, and now I have!"

Damaris said, "You look much better now, Esther."

"The twins said it must have been Beulah who told my uncle."

Damaris screwed up her face. "Beulah would. She always does everything perfectly."

"She never turns up her skirt, either," said Charity. "And she wears her head scarf all the way to school."

"Does Eli want to marry her?"

Damaris shrugged. "Eli is stupid. She will make all the decisions and boss him around and say it is what he has told her. When she is with child she will say, 'My husband says I must take care. He will not let me cook the meal. He says I have to rest.'"

"Will he cook, if she won't?" I asked. Uncle Caleb wouldn't know a pot from a frying pan.

They giggled. "Heavens no! He is a man. No, one of us girls will have to go round to her house and cook the meal for her."

"She mightn't be able to have kids," I said. If Eli was that wet he probably wouldn't know he had to do something other than hold her hand.

"It is unkind to wish that she be barren," Damaris said gently.

God, I *hate* being so goddamned good!

At school, Ms. Chandler asked me for a note. "For being away yesterday," she said sharply.

"I'm sorry, I didn't think. Can I bring it tomorrow?"

"Very well." She straightened up. "It isn't a good start, Esther, to be absent on the second day of term. Were you ill?"

Suddenly I'd had it up to my eyeballs with people telling me off. "No." I lifted my chin and glared at her. "My uncle objected to me cutting my hair off. He made me stay in the discipline room all day and learn psalms off by heart. Do you want to hear them?"

All the fight went out of her. "I'm sorry, Esther. And no, I don't want to hear them—and I'll get off your back. Bring me a note if you can."

Wow! That was a turnaround, for sure.

"You should not have said that," Damaris whispered. "We are not permitted to discuss home with our teachers."

"Are you going to tell?" I hissed back.

"Certainly not. It is a matter between you and your conscience."

That was something, anyway.

Mrs. Fletcher came and asked me to pop out of class for a minute. "Just to let you know I've ruled out the Red Cross and a couple of other organizations she could have been working for. Still trying, don't give up hope." She flicked at my hair. "Tough day, yesterday?" I nodded. "Let me know if things get too difficult. Promise?"

I nodded again. "It's okay. I just lost my temper."

"Never mind, the hair suits you."

It was a good day at school. We had P.E. You can't imagine what heaven it was to get into the shorts and T-shirt. All the other girls were moaning about how gross they were and how we should be allowed to wear whatever we wanted. I glanced at Damaris and Charity. Charity whispered, "I would not want to do P.E. in a long skirt!"

I went to my option classes for the first time. Uncle Caleb had chosen them for me, and as near as he could, he'd chosen cooking, cleanliness, and godliness. I was to study food technology and home economics. I wanted to learn Japanese and graphics.

I collected Maggie and the boys after school and went home. The twins had made Aunt Naomi go to bed. She looked dreadful. "Would you like me to ask Uncle Caleb to come home?" I asked her. "Should you go to the doctor?"

She shook her head. "No, Esther. I will be all right. I am just a little tired."

The twins and Maggie helped me cook dinner. Uncle Caleb came home earlier than usual and went straight in to Aunt Naomi. He stayed there for ages, and we could hear him praying. "I think she should see a doctor," I said to Daniel.

"She is my mother, and I cannot do anything," he said softly, as if to himself.

"Do you know what you're going to do?" I asked, after glancing around to make sure nobody was listening.

He nodded. "Yes, but I will not do it while my mother is unwell."

"Be careful," I said. "You can always find a reason for not doing something as difficult as that."

He stared at me, and after an age he whispered, "You are right. First it was Miriam, then it was Magdalene, now it is my mother."

Aunt Naomi didn't come to the evening prayer session that night. "She is resting," was all my gray uncle would say. We prayed for her and the baby.

Before he went to work the next day Uncle Caleb gave Rebecca a note. "Take it to Aunt Adah, daughter. She will come at lunchtime to check on your mother."

He looked at the children's anxious faces. "Do not worry. I have prayed to the Lord. All will be well."

Somehow, I managed to keep my mouth shut.

"Aunt, are you sure?" I asked before I left for school.

"Your uncle has prayed for me. He is confident that all will be well." She didn't look quite so confident to me. I put a jug of lemon cordial on the table beside her. "Thank you, Esther. You are very thoughtful," she whispered. She'd thanked me!

I went off to school with Charity and Damaris. "I'm worried about her," I told them. "She should see a doctor. I think she should be in hospital."

"It does you credit," Damaris smiled at me. "But it is not your place to question your uncle's judgment. He has prayed, and God has led him to the correct path of action."

Holy cow. A whole, stampeding herd of bloody holy cows. I stopped abruptly and turned around. "I'm going to stay with her. She shouldn't be by herself."

"Esther!" Charity called after me. "Your uncle will be severely displeased! It is not your place to do this!"

I ignored her. What had Mrs. Fletcher said?

Something about being able to live with myself being a reasonably important concept.

I tiptoed into Aunt Naomi's room. "Aunt? I am going to stay with you today."

She turned her head and whispered, "Thank you, Esther. I do not feel very well, it will be good to have you here."

That frightened me. She was actually admitting to not feeling well. I thought she must be nearly dying. "Should I get a doctor?" I whispered.

"No. I will try to sleep a little. I am glad you are here."

I sat beside her bed and for something to do I hemmed more of Beulah's dumb napkins. And I didn't tie the cotton. I longed for a book. Or a telly. Or a radio. And my mother.

After about an hour, Aunt Naomi started moaning and tossing her head around on the pillow. I went and got a cold, damp cloth to put on her forehead. She didn't stop. I tried to wake her up, but she didn't seem to be conscious.

I jumped up, my heart beating hard somewhere in my throat. I had to get help and get it fast. I ran to the neighbor's place. Nobody home. Nor at the next place. Oh God, what should I do? A car was coming down the road. I ran out and waved madly, yelling, "Stop! Please stop and help me!"

It stopped, and a man stuck his head out. "What's up, kid?"

"It's my aunt," I gabbled. "I think she's dying, and there's no phone!"

He had a cell phone! He punched in 111 and handed it to me. "Ambulance!" I cried when the voice asked what service I wanted.

"We'll come right away," they said. "Don't worry, we'll be there."

"Oh, thank you!" I handed the phone back to the man.

"You want me to come in and wait with you?"

I did, I really did, but I shook my head. "My aunt would be upset. She is very religious, and she would think it was wrong." Don't ask me why.

He just nodded. "Okay, then. Hope she'll be all right."

I ran back to the house. She still didn't answer me when I talked to her, and her face was paler than before. Hurry!

They came, they did come. Two of them. They wore uniforms and carried bags. Best of all, they knew what to do. "In here," I cried, leading the way.

"My aunt is in here."

The big man with the beard told me his name was Tony. "How long has she been sick?" He took something out of his bag, turned Aunt Naomi on her side, and slid the thing into her mouth.

I tried to think. "Sunday. She didn't seem very well on Sunday."

The other man kept bringing gear in. There were two machines with TV-type screens. An oxygen bottle. They put a mask over her face. A drip into her arm. They worked quickly, talking quietly and asking me questions I couldn't answer. "What date is the baby due?"

"March, I think," I faltered. "I'm not sure."

"You're not sure?" I could hear all sorts of comments in that one question.

"It's the religion," I said desperately. "They prayed. They said she'd be all right. They won't tell me anything."

"She'll have to have a cesarean," Tony said. "Will that be a problem?"

I shook my head. "No. I don't think so."

"Good. We'll take her to hospital. Can you come? We'll need to know how to contact her husband."

Gently, they lifted her onto a stretcher. I watched

their faces. Tony had his lips pinched together, and he was frowning.

I climbed in the back of the ambulance. "Sit there," he said, pointing at a little seat behind the driver. He sat beside her head.

"She's very sick, isn't she?" I whispered.

"Yes, but we'll have her to hospital double-quick." As he said it, the ambulance moved and the siren shrieked. The driver was talking into the radio, but I couldn't hear because of the partition between us.

"What's wrong with her?" I asked. "My uncle won't tell me. He'll say I don't need to know—but I do!" And so will Daniel.

Without taking his eyes from Aunt Naomi, he told me. "She's very ill. It's called preeclamptic toxemia." He nodded in the direction of the driver. "John's radioed the hospital to tell them to have specialists waiting. They'll take her straight to surgery."

The siren wailed somewhere above my head. "They only use the siren when it's real bad, don't they?"

"Yes," he said gently, "that's right. You'd best be prepared. This is an extreme emergency. Your aunt is very, very ill."

I started shaking. Aunt Naomi was dying. Uncle Caleb would kill me, whatever happened. He'd say it was the will of God, and who did I think I was to question that?

We got to the hospital, and they had her out of the ambulance almost before it had stopped. I climbed out and stood beside it. Where should I go? What should I do? At last, Tony came back. He took my arm and led me inside to a waiting room. "They're looking after her. How do we get hold of her husband?" I told him where Uncle Caleb worked, and a woman went away to ring him.

"You did well, lassie. All we can do now is wait."

Uncle Caleb would have prayed. I didn't. I waited. There were magazines, but I couldn't look at them. I sat on a hard chair and tried to stop shivering. It must have only been about fifteen minutes before Uncle Caleb strode in. "My wife? Where is she?"

A nurse led him away. He hadn't even seen me, and I have to admit I was glad. Somebody touched my arm. Daniel. I jumped up and threw my arms around him. "Oh, Daniel, I'm so pleased to see you!"

He actually hugged me back. "How is it that you knew she was ill? You were at school!"

I told him what I'd done. "Uncle Caleb will kill me," I said dismally.

Daniel was silent for a long time, then at last he said, "This has shown me I cannot live this way, Kirby. I knew my mother needed help. I told my father, but he said he had prayed, and all would be well. So I did nothing. It was not my place." He turned to look at me. "If you had thought the same way, then my mother would have no chance of life. She might even be dead at this very moment."

"Daniel," I whispered, "she is very ill." I told him everything the ambulance man had told me. I even remembered the words: *preeclamptic toxemia.*

His face turned white, and he put his arm around me. I don't know if it was to comfort himself or me, but it helped.

"Thank you for what you did, Kirby," he said. "I could not have borne it if my mother had died there, alone." He breathed in, choking a little. "I knew she was too ill to leave. I knew it."

It was a long time before Uncle Caleb came back. We stood up and went toward him. Could tell nothing from his face.

"Is she . . ." Daniel couldn't finish the sentence.

"She is very ill, but they think she will recover. We and the Fellowship will pray for her."

My legs gave way and I collapsed onto a chair.

Uncle Caleb looked at me gravely. "The Lord works in mysterious ways, Esther. You were the means by which He saved my wife. We will pray and give thanks when we return home."

I didn't say anything. What could you say?

"The child?" Daniel asked. "What of the baby?"

"The child is ill. It is a girl, and she is being cared for. I have seen her and blessed her."

"Father, what happened? What made my mother so ill? She has never been ill before with a baby."

Uncle Caleb rubbed a hand across his forehead— the first time I'd ever seen him do anything like that. "Daniel, you know we are not concerned by such questions. All that concerns us is that the Lord has been pleased to spare your mother. The fate of your sister is still in His hands. We will pray for the strength to accept His will." Daniel bowed his head, but I could feel the tension in him, see the set of his shoulders.

"May we visit my aunt?" I whispered, still expecting a lecture on disobedience, transgression, and iniquity.

"You may go and say a prayer by her bedside," he said, after thinking about it. "She is unconscious still from the operation."

We trailed behind Uncle Caleb to where Aunt Naomi was lying. Daniel and I stared at the drip and the tubes.

We had to stand with our heads bowed while he intoned a prayer. The nurse monitoring the machines connected to her glanced at him, but she stayed where she was and didn't bow her head. Aunt Naomi lay like a wax statue. But she was still alive. Because of me. Handmaiden of the Lord.

Hadn't my uncle heard that the Lord helps those who help themselves?

I wanted to see the baby. We tiptoed into the neonatal unit and stared down at a tiny body hitched up to tubes and lying naked, except for a nappy, in an incubator.

"She is so small," Daniel breathed.

"She's a fighter," I murmured. "She's got to be!"

"It is not up to her," my uncle said. "It is the will of the Lord."

"What is her name?" Daniel asked, his eyes glued to his baby sister.

"I have named her Zillah."

"Zillah," Daniel repeated, only when he said it, it sounded like a caress.

That night after dinner we had the granddaddy of a prayer session. Many people from the church came, and there was singing, with Bible readings and prayers. The women brought baking and casseroles so that we girls wouldn't have to cook for days.

I let my thoughts wander. When was Daniel going to drop his bombshell? I couldn't blame him for not wanting to raise the question right now. All the children were upset, and it damned well didn't help that Uncle Caleb wouldn't tell them anything useful.

When I put Maggie to bed, I asked the twins to come and help me. I told them everything I knew. I told them how I hadn't gone to school. I especially told them that so they could see it was sometimes a good idea to use your own brain. "Will our sister die?" Maggie asked, her face pale and scared.

I gave her a huge hug. "She might. She is very tiny and she isn't very well."

"Will she go to heaven if she dies—or will she be like Miriam?" Maggie asked.

"Miriam didn't die," I said. "Miriam ran away, and she is alive and well and living in Wellington." I took a deep breath. "Zillah is very sick and very small. If she dies, she will go to heaven."

"Esther," said Rachel, "do you think the Lord sent your mother to Africa so that you could come here and save our mother?"

"The Lord might know that," I said, "but I sure don't." And they might as well get used to the idea that I wasn't going to stay. "I want my mother to come home—and when she does, I will go and live with her."

Silence. Then Rebecca whispered, "We will miss you."

"I don't want you to go!" Maggie wailed. Great, Kirby—you sure know when to pick your times.

"I can't stay here," I told Maggie as gently as I could. "I'm different. I don't believe the same things you do. I get into trouble and make people unhappy. It'll be better when I've gone."

"We will all miss you," said Rachel, blinking away tears.

That night I dreamed of Aunt Naomi lying dead and a baby crying and crying and there were long, polished corridors and I couldn't find her or the baby. In the morning I rushed out and asked Uncle Caleb how Aunt Naomi was.

"I have been up to the hospital," he said. "She is making progress and the child still lives." That was good. Very good. And I was impressed. He'd actually gone up to the hospital before seven in the morning. Perhaps he did love her in his own peculiar way.

I asked him if he would write me a note to explain why I was absent yesterday. I read it when he went out of the room: *Please excuse Esther's absence yesterday. She was doing the Lord's work.*

7

MS. CHANDLER'S EYEBROWS HIT HER hairline when she read the note. "Are you able to tell me just what the Lord's work was, Esther?"

I glanced at Damaris and Charity who were watching me with serious faces. "My aunt was taken to hospital and had an emergency cesarean," I said.

Ms. Chandler gave me a hard look that said, *And what's the rest of the story?* but all she said aloud was, "I wish her a speedy recovery."

It was hard to keep my mind on things that day. My thoughts kept whizzing off to Mum, and then I'd find myself thinking about Aunt Naomi and

Zillah. Then Daniel would swim into the picture. Altogether I was relieved when the bell went for hometime.

"We will pray for Aunt Naomi and the baby," said Damaris.

"And for you," Charity said. "You are worried in your soul."

A little diversion occurred that evening. I got my period for the first time since I'd been in that house. "Where does Aunt Naomi keep the pads?" I asked the twins. I somehow couldn't imagine she'd have tampons.

They stared at me. "Writing pads?" Rebecca asked.

"No, dopey! For when you get your period. Pads. Or tampons."

More blank stares. "What do you mean? What are tampons?" Rachel asked finally.

Well, it didn't surprise me that Aunt Naomi didn't use tampons. Too modern altogether. "Pads then," I said. "You know—so that you won't bleed all over your underpants. I've got my period," I explained patiently.

"But what do you mean?" Rebecca demanded. "You are speaking in riddles, Esther!"

They didn't know what periods were. So I told

them. "And I need pads," I said, "or I'll have blood all over my skirt."

They were stunned and didn't know whether to believe me or not. And they were no help. Which left me with a bit of a problem. I stuffed toilet paper in my underpants until I could think what to do. Luckily, Aunt Dorcas came over with bags of groceries and I explained the problem to her.

"Sister Naomi will have provisions put aside in the linen cupboard. I will look, if you like." She went to the linen cupboard and fished out squares of white toweling, an elastic waistband, and a couple of safety pins. "Here you are." She smiled and explained how to fold them and how to soak the used towels in cold water.

"I can't use these!" I said, horrified.

"There is nothing else to use," she pointed out.

"Can't I buy some pads or tampons?"

"We do not use such things," she said, and that was that.

The only good news in the entire day was that Aunt Naomi was a little better and the baby was still alive.

On the way to the bus stop the next morning I told Damaris and Charity about how the twins

didn't know what a period was. And guess what—
I got blank stares from them as well. Nobody had
told those girls about getting their period, and they
were both nearly fourteen.

"Do you know how babies are made?" I asked.

"When a man embraces his wife in the marriage
bed," Charity said.

"You haven't a clue, have you?"

They shook their heads. "I have often wondered," Damaris whispered, looking around in case
God was waiting to hit her over the head.

"Shall I tell you?"

They thought about that. "I would like to know,"
Damaris said at last. "But we will have to decide if it
is a godly thing to know. Our parents would tell us
if they wanted us to know."

That evening, Daniel was allowed to visit Aunt
Naomi while Uncle Caleb went to a special prayer
meeting for her recovery. When Daniel came back,
the children and I crowded around him. "Sit down,"
he said, "and I will tell you everything." We sat
around the table.

"Our mother is still very sick. She can only speak
in a whisper. She said to tell you all that she is looking forward to coming home again."

"Can we go and visit her?" Abraham demanded.

Daniel shook his head. "Not yet. She gets very tired. I could only stay for two minutes."

"What about the baby?" asked Maggie. "Can the baby come home?"

Daniel picked her up and hugged her. "The doctors are worried about Zillah. They do not know if she will live. They might have to operate."

"Shall we pray for her?" Rachel asked, her face pale.

"That would be a good idea," said Daniel. They all bowed their heads and he said a simple prayer for his tiny sister. "Praise the Lord," the others responded.

Dorcas came around that night to see that things were running smoothly. "You will remember to cook for the Meet this Sabbath," she said as she ran an eye over the ironing Rebecca was doing.

"What meat?" I asked.

Rachel jumped in, "It is a big meeting and everyone goes and . . ."

Dorcas stopped her. "That will do, Rachel." To me, she said, "Every three months, the community meets to decide matters of importance. This meeting is particularly important because the elders will decide whether we will all move to Nelson to join the community there."

I stopped scrubbing carrots and stared at her. I'd forgotten about that. "Move to Nelson?" Away from Mrs. Fletcher? Away from an ordinary school?

Dorcas nodded briskly. "Many of us feel it would be a most positive move. You are dripping muddy water on your apron, Esther! You should make an apple shortcake and a fruit salad for the Meet." With that, she bustled off.

Maggie was bursting with news. "Esther! I can go to the Meet now! I am five! I am old enough to go to the Meet!"

"Great!" I hugged her absentmindedly. "So who looks after the little ones?"

Rebecca giggled. "The next three girls to be married. Beulah and Susannah and Judith."

"And it will be so exciting this time," Rebecca added, shaking water over one of Uncle Caleb's shirts to dampen it. "It is Damaris's fourteenth birthday in April, and they will hold the betrothal negotiations at this Meet and the actual betrothal at the next one."

"And everyone knows she is promised to Daniel!" Rachel danced around, folding tea towels into tidy squares.

"What about Daniel?" I asked. "Daniel might not want to marry her. He might not want to marry when he's so young." I wanted to say more, but I couldn't, not without making a whole lot more trouble for him.

"They will not marry for two years," Rachel pointed out. "Daniel will be nineteen and a half by then." Her tone suggested that was practically ancient.

I rubbed at the dirty mark on my apron. "That's much too young to be married. I'm not going to get married until I'm thirty. If I get married at all."

They stared at me, but we heard Uncle Caleb's car in the drive, and that was the finish of chatting.

In the middle of the night, I heard a strange sound. It was a telephone. I thought I was dreaming, but it kept ringing. I sat up and slid from my bed. It was! It was a telephone and in this house. I knew I was awake, because I twisted my little toe when I slid out of bed, and it hurt.

I followed the sound. There was a light in Uncle Caleb's room. He was standing beside the bed, dressed in pajamas out of the ark and staring at a mobile phone as if it was a deadly snake.

"Answer it!" I ran toward him.

He spread his hands. "I do not understand how to use it."

I snatched it up, pressed the talk button. "Hello?" I gasped.

It was the hospital. Of course. Who else? "May I speak to Mr. Pilgrim, please."

I handed the phone over. He took it, holding it with a thumb and one finger. "Yes? I see. I will come."

He handed me back the phone, and I switched it off. "They insisted I take it tonight," he said. "In case they had to contact me. Please leave me, Esther. I must go to the hospital."

"But what is wrong?" I whispered, not really believing he would go and not tell me.

He was walking toward the wardrobe, but he paused, thought for three whole seconds, then said, "It is your sister. There is a crisis. They wish to operate."

I left the room, but I didn't go back to bed. I watched the car lights slice through the night. Little Zillah. She was so tiny. *Please God, keep her safe*.

I stopped. That was a prayer. I had prayed. Me, who didn't believe in God. I sank down on the window seat, wanting my mother, longing for my ordinary, everyday, crazy life. Who was I now? Who I used to be was disappearing, and there were only bits of me left that sometimes I caught sight of in puddles or dark windows.

8

ZILLAH HUNG ON TO LIFE.

"May I take the children to see her?" Daniel asked the next evening.

"That would not be a good idea," said Uncle Caleb. How he could say that when they were all staring at him with eyes that begged, I didn't know.

"With respect, Father," Daniel said, "do you not feel it would help them all if they could see how very small she is?"

Not one of those kids said a word. But not even Uncle Caleb could pretend they weren't interested in seeing their sister. "I will pray about it," he said at last, and bowed his head.

It was all I could do to keep my mouth shut. I wasn't too impressed by his last effort at asking for guidance. However, this time apparently the Lord said it was okay.

"Thank you, Father!" from each kid.

"Can I take her a flower?" asked Abraham. "Just a little one, because she is little."

Before his father could answer, Daniel smiled at Abraham and said, "I do not think flowers would be allowed in the nursery where she is. But take one and we will give it to our mother to keep for Zillah."

"May we see Mother, too?" Rebecca asked, her face alight.

Again, they turned to their father for permission. "If the hospital allows it," he said—without praying about it.

We climbed into the car—a red Honda this time. Abraham carried a small pink rosebud and two white daisies. Uncle Caleb didn't come, so the children chattered the way kids are supposed to. "Why did she need an operation?" Rachel asked.

"What is an operation?" Luke asked.

"Does it hurt?" Maggie's eyes were wide and scared.

"How do babies get born without an operation?"

The real curly one. From Rebecca.

Daniel was suddenly very busy driving carefully around a corner.

"They come out a special hole between the mother's legs," I answered for him.

"But that would hurt!" Rachel cried.

"So everybody says."

We got to the hospital before anyone asked how the baby got in there in the first place. Now that would really have been interesting. And I reckon Daniel could have fielded that one. Then I wondered if he knew himself.

I asked him as the kids raced up to the hospital from the car park. He actually laughed, then smiled again at my astonished face. "Yes, I do. But I had to spend three whole days in the discipline room because of it."

"Huh? How come?"

"We are supposed to be excused from any class to do with reproduction. I stayed, but Beulah found out, and she told my father. But it was too late by then, because I had the knowledge."

I looked at him with admiration. "What a little rebel you are!"

The children quieted the moment we walked

inside the hospital. No one said anything as we tip-toed into the neonatal ward. A nurse led us to Zillah's incubator. "Here she is, your little sister." She smiled at our anxious faces. "She's doing well. The operation was a success. We're very pleased with her."

Luke reached out toward the incubator. "But she has got no clothes on! Is she cold?"

"Is she the smallest baby in the world?" Rebecca whispered.

The nurse was kind. She answered all our questions, and she let us stay there far longer than Uncle Caleb would have thought seemly. Then she took us in to Aunt Naomi. "Only a little visit," she warned. "Your mother is not very strong yet."

She was looking a heap better than when I'd seen her last. She smiled at the kids and stretched out a hand. "It is good to see you. Very good." One at a time, they went up to her and kissed her cheek.

"Mother," the words burst from Maggie, "did the doctor sew you up with herringbone stitch?"

Aunt Naomi actually smiled. "I do not think so, Magdalene." She reached for Maggie's hand. "Now tell me about school. Do you like it?"

We stayed for about five minutes before Daniel

said, "Mother is getting tired. We will say good-bye now."

So they kissed her again. "Thank you, Daniel," she murmured. "You are a good son."

"Ouch," I whispered to him when we were outside.

"I love them," he said fiercely. "I love them so much. I do not want to leave." Our shoes squeaked on the floor, and I heard the swishing of my dumb skirt. "But I cannot stay."

It was Friday the next day, and Charity and Damaris were full of the Meet. "How come you're not getting betrothed, too?" I asked Charity.

"I have asked for an extra year before I am married," she said. "We are permitted to do that."

Damaris giggled. "That is because she thought she might have to marry Eli."

Charity shook her head. "No it is not. Do not be unkind, Damaris."

"So why, then?" I asked. The rest of them seemed all fired keen on getting hitched as soon as they could.

"Jonas and I have discussed it, and we both prefer to marry when we are older."

Seventeen was older? What if she still didn't want to get married when she was seventeen?

Mrs. Fletcher asked to see me, and Beulah caught me as I was on my way to her office. "You should be in class," she said, giving me the evils.

"So should you."

"I have been to the dentist," she said. "What is your excuse?"

"I'm going to the doctor. For an abortion." That shut her up. She went an ugly pink and flounced off with her drippy uniform dragging around her ankles. If she told Uncle Caleb, then I'd deny it, and he just might believe me, and then she would get prayed over. Cow. Unholy cow.

Mrs. Fletcher gave me a hug and then held on to my shoulders and looked hard at me. "How's it all going?"

So I told her everything from Zillah to Daniel to Damaris and Beulah. It made me realize how much I missed being able to rabbit on to my friends and to Mum. Especially Mum.

"Have you found anything out about Mum?" I asked.

She didn't answer straight away and I sat up, staring at her. "What's wrong? Mrs. Fletcher, you have to tell me, what's wrong?"

She patted my arm. "Nothing's wrong, Kirby.

Calm down. It's just that things aren't quite right, either." She sat back in her chair, her eyes on my face. "I haven't been able to find any trace of your mother, my dear. One of the organizations said she'd been on their list of nurses who had applied to go and work in refugee camps, but that she hadn't actually gone."

I stared at her. "But she wrote to me! I had a letter. An airmail letter with a Z in the postmark. Look, I'll show you!" I carried it with me everywhere. I scrabbled in my bag and held it out.

Mrs. Fletcher read the letter, turned it over, and examined the postmark. "Kirby—I think that Z is the Z in *New Zealand*."

"But she's in Africa!"

Mrs. Fletcher took hold of both my hands firmly. "Listen, Kirby. I think she meant to go to Africa, but as far as I can tell, she isn't there." She gave my hands a little shake. "She must be somewhere, and we'll find her. Don't worry."

I couldn't take in what she was saying. I felt weak and dizzy and sick. If she wasn't in Africa, where was she? And why?

"But the letter," I whispered again. "She says the people are dedicated and the conditions are appalling. She is there. She is!" But even as I said it, I felt hollow with doubt.

"Anybody could have written those things," Mrs. Fletcher said gently.

"But why?" I felt as if the words were being torn out of my heart. "She loves me! Why would she try to hide from me?"

"We'll find her. It's not so easy to disappear."

"Unless she's dead." I had to say it.

"I think you'd have heard if she'd died," Mrs. Fletcher said. She looked as if she was going to say something else, but when she didn't I just shook my head. No energy left to argue and plead. I was made of cotton wool, an unreal child to be endured.

Somebody knocked urgently on Mrs. Fletcher's door. Somewhere, a million miles away from me, I could hear her talking to a boy whose words tripped over themselves. Then she was shaking my shoulder. "I have to go. Another crisis. I'll keep working on it, Kirby. Stay here as long as you need."

But I didn't want to sit there by myself with questions I couldn't answer whizzing around in my head.

I went back to class. It was cooking, even though it said *Food Technology* on my timetable. I tried to think about other things. Like Uncle Caleb choosing my options for me—as if I didn't get enough cooking experience already. Would he know if I swapped to graphics? Dumb question. Ira was doing graphics and Ira was more poisonous than Beulah. The Elders loved him. I walked into the cooking room, and I must've looked bad, because Mrs. East didn't even ask me for a late note. She just gave me a sharp glance then sent me off to help Charity, Damaris, and another girl make something that involved melting butter and sugar together.

"Esther!"

I jumped. Oh my God! I'd set the stove on fire! Mrs. East grabbed a fire extinguisher and doused it. I leaned on the sink and laughed, turned around so my back was against it, and slid down the cupboards until I was sitting on the floor, my arms wrapped around my knees, and I laughed and laughed. Great gasps of laughter that hurt my chest and my throat.

Mrs. East threw a glass of cold water in my face. I heard her telling somebody to go for Mrs. Fletcher. Then Charity and Damaris were beside me, hauling me to my feet. I remember Mrs. Fletcher coming, but I was so tired. She took me to the sick bay, and

I slept through most of the day. She came and sat on my bed in the afternoon.

"I think it's time to get you out of there," she said.

I sat up. "No! I do not want to leave. Not yet. Daniel . . . and I want to tell Maggie . . . and the twins." I couldn't leave. I'd be nobody. A nothing. Not Esther and not Kirby. And I'd have nobody. No Maggie, no family. No mother.

She looked at me, her face serious. "Take another week, if you want. But ask yourself this: who are you—Esther or Kirby?"

I flopped down away from her and put my arm over my face. Could she see into my mind? "I am Kirby. I am not Esther." Somebody else was saying that. Somebody who didn't believe the words coming out of her mouth. Mrs. Fletcher didn't believe them either. She stroked the hair away from my face just the way Mum would have done.

"No?" she asked. "Since when did Kirby speak like that? Kirby would've said *I'm* and *I'm not*." She stood up. "Don't leave it too long, Kirby. And remember, I'm here if you need me."

Damaris and Charity came to collect me when the last bell went. "Are you well?" Charity asked, anxious.

I nodded. "Yes, I'm fine." They were both staring at me with worried faces. I took a deep breath. "Mrs. Fletcher told me that . . ." I stopped. Tried again. "She said she hasn't been able to trace my mother. I'm worried about her. I don't know where she is."

Damaris hugged me—and that was against the Rule. "We will pray for her."

"Thanks," I muttered. I wished I could tell them everything. I wished I could talk about Mum, and I wished I could tell them I was feeling torn in two, that Esther was sometimes more real than Kirby and how much that frightened me.

I collected Maggie and the boys from school. Their chatter made me feel more like myself again— but which self, I wasn't quite sure.

I longed to talk to Daniel about Mum, but he wasn't home. "You look funny, Esther," said Rachel. "Are you all right?"

"Are you going to die?" asked Maggie.

I poured her a drink of lemon cordial from the jug the twins had put on the table. They all watched me, and not one of them touched the food in front of them, not even Abraham. I sat down. "I am upset," I said carefully. "I found out today that my mother didn't go to Africa, like she said she was going to."

"She told a lie?" Abraham's eyes sparkled at the thought of an adult doing something that wicked.

Rebecca waved a hand to shush him. "Do you know where she is?"

I shook my head. Maggie threw herself into my lap and flung her arms around my neck. "Do not cry, Esther!"

"But she wrote to Father," Rachel said, frowning.

"You can't ask him," said Abraham, reaching for a biscuit. "He'd be so angry."

Neither of the twins corrected his language. "What will you do?" Rebecca asked.

"I want to find her," I said.

"Will you go away? Do not go away!" Maggie and Luke said together.

I hugged Maggie gently. "I will have to." I looked at the twins and Abraham and Luke. "I can't stay here. I've got to find my mother and . . ." I stopped. How could I tell them I had to find myself before it was too late and I vanished, worn away under a welter of prayers, rules, and restrictions.

"Don't go!" Maggie sobbed. "Don't die!"

I tightened my arms around her. "When I go," I told the twins, "you have to talk to her about it. Remind her I'm not dead. Tell her Miriam's not dead." They didn't say anything. "Promise!" I shouted.

"It is against the Rule," Rachel said at last.

I jumped up, Maggie still clinging to me, and I stared down at them. "So break it! It's wicked! She's too little to understand. Your father doesn't have to know."

The twins turned from me and looked at each other. Finally Rebecca said, "We will think about it, Esther. That is all we can promise. It will grieve the Lord and it will grieve our parents if we break the Rule."

With an effort I sat down again. It wasn't their fault. "Thank you," I muttered, trying to smile.

The next day, the girls and I had to clean the house so well it's a wonder it didn't fall down. Windows, ceilings, door frames, skirting boards, the whole darned lot. And why? Because the bloody men had decided that's what had to be done before every Meet. The only good thing about it was that it stopped my mind from worrying endlessly about Mum.

While we cleaned, Uncle Caleb disappeared into his study, and Daniel sat with Abraham and Luke and took them for Bible study.

"Don't let it strain your brain," I said, letting water drip on his head as I swiped the mop at the ceiling.

"This is the Rule," he answered in a flat voice.

"Sorry," I muttered, and got a quick half smile in return.

Then something totally out of the ordinary happened. There was a knock on the door. Normally, when another member of the faith came to the house, they came straight in and called out, "Praise the Lord."

Nobody knocked on the door.

"I will get Father," Abraham said. Any excuse to escape from Bible study.

"Don't bother," I said. "It'll just be somebody selling something. I'll tell them to go away." Daniel was talking as I walked to the door, but I didn't really listen.

I opened the door to find a guy standing there. "We don't want any, thanks," I said.

He grinned. "I'm not selling. I'm looking for Kirby Greenland."

I gasped, but before I could answer, Uncle Caleb was beside me and saying, "Go into the house, Esther."

"But Uncle . . . that's me! He's asking for me!" I whirled around to the man, "Is it Mum? You know something about my mother?"

"Go inside, Esther," my uncle said again. "I will deal with this." He stepped between us so that I couldn't see the man and he stood there, his eyes boring through me.

"Uncle Caleb, please!" I whispered.

Daniel had come to the door. "Father, with your permission, I will escort Esther into the house. We will study the Scripture together for an hour."

After about ten seconds, Uncle Caleb nodded. "Thank you, Daniel. Will you also explain to your sister the impropriety of answering the door herself?"

"Yes, Father."

Daniel stood back and motioned with his arm for me to go back into the house. He frowned and gave his head a tiny shake when I opened my mouth to protest. So I shut it again and went inside. It was one of the hardest things I've done in my life. That man knew something about my mother, and Uncle Caleb wouldn't tell me, not even if hell froze over. Especially not then.

"Wow!" Abraham whispered. "I bet you're for

the discipline room tomorrow!"

Daniel pulled out a chair for me at the table. "Do you think," he said to Abraham, "that your words were seemly?"

Abraham grinned. "No, but Father can't put us both in the discipline room."

"I think," said Daniel, "that some discipline is needed for you right now. You will clean the windows in our bedroom. Go now, if you please."

It wasn't really a punishment. We all knew Abraham would far rather do something active than sit around studying scripture. "Girls' work!" he said, but he went off cheerfully enough. Luke sighed, but stayed where he was.

Daniel then explained to me about answering the door. "A woman never answers a knock on the door. It is not seemly. She has no way of knowing what she may be exposing herself or her family to."

"Thank you, Daniel. I understand now." We both spoke in flat voices, saying words we didn't mean. Our eyes asked questions neither of us knew answers to.

Uncle Caleb came back inside. Daniel kicked my foot. I jumped up and bowed my head. "Uncle Caleb, please excuse my transgression. I did not understand that I was breaking the Rule." *Who was he? Did he have news about Mum?* I'd taken the breath to ask, when Daniel's hand clenched on my wrist.

"Your transgression is excused, Esther. We will pray tonight for forgiveness. And in the meantime, please continue your housework." He marched off to the study.

"You were supposed to read with us for an hour," Luke said accusingly.

Daniel smiled at him, but when he spoke, the words were for me. "I think our father has things on his mind."

That night I had dreams about Mum. She was walking across a desert, and she was thirsty. I remember that I woke up, crying. Then the next thing I knew Uncle Caleb was standing beside my bed calling my name. "Esther! Wake up. It is time to get up and prepare the food for the Meet."

Bloody hell, it was only five o'clock. I slid down from the bunk, careful not to say anything or do anything that would get me shut in the discipline room for the day. I'd had time to realize it was only because Daniel had come to my rescue yesterday that I was free now.

However, I didn't totally get away with answering

the door. Uncle Caleb came and sat in the kitchen all the time I was cooking and he read bits of the Bible at me. He ranted at me about the Rule.

"Yes, Uncle Caleb," I said and chopped viciously at an apple.

"Praise the Lord," I said, thumping down on the pastry for the apple shortcake. *Tell me what that man wanted. Tell me about my mother.*

Not a word about that. Of course. What did I expect?

At seven o'clock, I woke the children. By eight o'clock, we were all packed into the car—a white Toyota—along with the shortcakes and salads. The dishes were done, the beds made, the house immaculate. Holy cow. Mum would never believe it. Was she still alive? Uncle Caleb must tell me if she wasn't. Surely?

The twins kept bouncing around, glancing at Daniel. He was driving, and his face was white and strained. Today he would have to agree to marry Damaris, or . . . what?

Could we run away together? What about Maggie? The twins? Who would take the boys to the park?

And Aunt Naomi. If Daniel got chucked out

today, she'd never see him again. Zillah would never know she had a sister called Miriam and a brother called Daniel. Or that once, for a little while, there had lived in their family a girl called . . . what? Esther? Kirby?

My fingers tightened on the salad bowl. Kirby. If I had to choose today as well, then I would choose to be Kirby.

We arrived at the Fellowship Center. Church. Why didn't they just call it a church? It was fragrant with flowers and bright with their colors. "Would you look after Maggie today?" I asked the twins.

"Of course," said Rebecca. "You will be busy in the kitchen."

Yeah. I'm a woman, so I get to make all the important decisions, like what plate the sliced lamb will go on. There was one good thing about it though, it got me out of the prayer sessions and singing, which went on all the morning. There were five of us in the kitchen—me, Damaris, Charity, Kezia, and a little waif called Talitha. Kezia bossed her around: "Talitha will set the tables." The worst job. "Talitha can fill the urn." The heaviest job.

"Drop dead, Kezia," I said finally. "You do the tables. Talitha can arrange the flowers."

"But Kezia always does them," Charity protested.

"Yeah, so why should she grab all the fun jobs and make Talitha do the bum stuff?" I demanded.

"I do not mind," Talitha whispered.

"Well, you should," I said. "You've got just as much right to enjoy life as she has!"

They stared at me; even Kezia shut her mouth. But Talitha was the first to move. She crept out to the dining hall and started setting the tables. I shrugged. Let her be a doormat. It was nothing to do with me. I was Kirby, not Esther.

The Meet bit didn't start until after lunch. I thought we'd miss the first bit while we did mountains of dishes. But there was music coming from the hall and a shuffling, thumping noise. "What are they doing?" I asked.

Kezia turned up her nose so she could look down it when she answered. "Dancing, of course."

I didn't believe it, but it was true. I opened the door a crack, and there in front of me was a whole hall full of weird people doing what looked horribly like line dancing. I wanted to shriek with laughter, but then I saw Maggie. She was between Daniel and Abraham, her face was lit up like a Christmas tree, and she was biting her bottom lip, she was concentrating so hard. Then I wanted to cry. Poor bloody little kid. Today for sure, she was going to lose her big brother.

I shut the door and went back to the dishes. Damaris was washing, but it was easy to see her mind wasn't on the job.

"Damaris! You are not getting these plates clean!" Kezia scolded.

Damaris jumped and water sloshed onto her apron. "I am sorry! I am finding it difficult to concentrate today!"

"I think you're crazy!" I burst out. "How can you even think about getting married! You're not even fourteen! You don't even get your period yet!"

She took her hands out of the soapy water and shook them. "You must speak for yourself, Esther, and not presume to speak for me." She dried her hands on a tea towel, carefully folded it, and put it back on the rail. "I have prayed about this, and it is the course my parents have chosen for me with love." She stared at me gravely. "It is you who are to be pitied, Esther. Deeply pitied."

Bloody hell.

We finished the dishes in silence with a great, gaping chasm between me and the four of them.

We changed our aprons for clean ones before we went out to join the rest of the community in the Place of Fellowship. Hall.

Each family sat together. There was a space beside Uncle Caleb to show that Aunt Naomi was with us in spirit. At least, that's what Rachel told me at afternoon tea. There was no space for Miriam. I sat between Daniel and Rebecca. Apparently we had to sit in order of age. I glanced at Maggie. She was still excited in spite of having spent the morning on her knees.

The leader whose name I couldn't remember stood on the stage, lifted his arms, and cut the talking dead. He was an old guy with a bit of white hair struggling for survival on his shiny head. "Brothers and sisters, we are gathered here today to discuss things of weight and import to our community. We have called on the Lord to bless our deliberations. Let us now begin. Will the Council of Elders please join me." What had Charity said, that day in the garden? Something about Damaris's grandfather being the leader. Old Baldy, therefore, had to be her grandpa. Ezra Faithful, his name was Ezra Faithful.

There were eleven empty chairs lined up on the stage. There was a bit of movement as the eleven

Elders made their way to the chairs. All men, of course. One empty chair. Only ten Elders.

I didn't have long to wonder who the other chair belonged to. Uncle Caleb. The first piece of business was whether he should be allowed to sit in it again.

An elder who had to be Damaris's father, because he had exactly the same eyebrows that tilted up at the ends, stood up and said, "Brothers and sisters. We must decide if our brother Caleb Pilgrim is fit to lead us again or whether he should be stood down forever from the Council of Elders. The loss of a daughter in such circumstances cannot help but call into question the devoutness of the family."

He'd been chucked out because of Miriam?

Beside me, Daniel sucked in a breath, and I could feel the stiffness of his arm against mine.

"Brother Caleb," commanded Old Baldy, "you may speak."

Uncle Caleb stood up and walked out to the front. "Brothers and sisters," he began, "my family has been visited by much affliction during these past months. We have all prayed to be cleansed of our impurities. We have repented of our transgressions. We ask only to be able to live according to the Rule. My brothers, I would willingly serve the community again as an Elder. But if it is the will of the Lord, I will serve with equal devotion and loyalty as an ordinary member."

I had to admire him. Everyone knew he loved being the boss, and here he was groveling on the floor and inviting them all to walk over him.

Dorcas's husband, I forget his name, stood up. "Brothers and sisters, I have prayed for guidance over this matter, and it has come to me that our Brother Caleb has much to offer this community. He should be allowed to serve us."

One by one, they stood up and said how the Lord had told them Brother Caleb was a right hot dude and ought to be allowed to work his butt off for them. Damaris's father was the only one the Lord had told different. But Old Baldy said, "Through the Elders, the Lord has spoken. We are pleased to readmit you to the rank of Elder, Brother Caleb."

Uncle Caleb got down on his knees and said, "I thank the Lord in His infinite wisdom. I promise to serve Him well."

Praise the Lord! Praise the Lord!

Daniel's arm gave a convulsive twitch.

The next piece of business was the move to Nelson. I felt sick. One by one, the Elders gave their opinion. Always starting with, "Brothers and Sisters, I have prayed to the Lord over this matter and it has come to me that . . ."

All the Elders were in favor of going. Uncle Caleb said, "The world is too much a part of the lives of our children, despite our best efforts. While our children must attend secular schools, we cannot hope to monitor their thoughts and deeds as we would wish."

Everybody knew about Miriam. There was a lot of nodding of heads and murmuring after he'd spoken. Old Baldy then invited the ordinary members to speak. Apparently this meant men only, and married men at that. Daniel made no attempt to offer an opinion. Even Thomasina's dorky husband was allowed to have his say—he had prayed, he said, and it had come to him that it would be better to stay in Wanganui because all the men had work here.

That went down like a dead duck. Apparently the Lord was going to get them all work in Nelson, too.

So they had another prayer after all the men had spoken. I was the only one who didn't bow my head. I was raging. What about the women? Didn't those guys care what their wives thought?

I managed to duck my head before Old Baldy came to the final *Praise the Lord*. I didn't want to be the one responsible for showing how wild the kids were because they went to ordinary schools.

It didn't matter. The Lord had decided the community would go to Nelson. They would all leave in three months and . . .

I didn't hear any more. Three months? We couldn't. I would have to leave school. What if Mrs. Fletcher still hadn't found Mum by then? The shock waves crashed in my brain and hurt my chest. And then I remembered—I was meant to be leaving in a week anyway. Why didn't it seem real?

We all stood up and sang. It was difficult to breathe. The high neck of my blouse choked me; my apron was too tight around my waist.

Daniel touched my hand briefly as we sat down again, but he didn't turn his head to look at me. Not with Ira sitting behind us.

We stopped then for afternoon tea. I helped put out cream sponge cakes and meringues. Sausage rolls and chocolate eclairs. Coffee cake and savory scones. Damaris poured tea with careful concentration. Three months. I saw my hands passing cups and saucers— hands that didn't seem to be connected to my arms.

Gideon came to get himself a cup of tea. He waited until Kezia was pouring, so that he had to be served by Damaris. "I wish you well, Sister Damaris," he said.

"I thank you, Brother Gideon," she whispered back.

And that was it. Except that Rebecca came rushing over, and not for tea, either. She'd already taken Uncle Caleb his. "What did he want?" she hissed at me.

I glanced at Damaris, who was biting her lip and refusing to look at Rebecca. "Take Daniel a cup of tea," I said, pouring one.

"He'll get his own," she snapped, still glaring at Damaris. "He's not married. Yet."

"Rebecca," I said, feeling so old that I creaked, "please take this to your brother. Tell him . . ." What could I say to tell him? "Tell him my thoughts are with him and tell him to remember Zillah."

"Why?" she demanded.

"Just do it. Please." I must've sounded as bad as I felt, because she took the cup and went.

We started washing cups and saucers. Damaris said nothing, and even Kezia kept her mouth shut.

The betrothal negotiations were next on the program.

"Brother Caleb," said Old Baldy when we'd all sat down again, "your son Daniel is of betrothal age. The community believes that Damaris Faithful will make him a fitting wife."

Uncle Caleb stood up. "As is the custom, I ask my son Daniel to speak his mind on this betrothal." He sat down and motioned Daniel to come up to the front.

Beside me, Daniel got slowly to his feet. He walked down the aisle, his shoes going *clunk, clunk* with every step. He climbed the two steps to the stage. Stood at the side of the row of Elders' chairs. Took a deep breath. "Father, brothers and sisters. I hold Damaris Faithful in high esteem. I know her to be pure in thought and deed. She upholds the Rule and she is good, kind, and seemly."

I slid a glance sideways. Apparently this was what normally happened. People were smiling and nodding, except Gideon, who looked like he was about to leap up and strangle Daniel. I couldn't see Damaris.

"However," Daniel continued in such a quiet voice that we had to strain to hear it. The silence deepened with that one word. *However* definitely wasn't in the script. Uncle Caleb's eyebrows had snapped together. "However, I ask to be stood down from marriage negotiations at this point."

"You are of age," huffed Old Baldy, "and you have already been given the extra year. Enlighten us as to your reasons, if you please." His voice cut the air with slivers of sharp ice. I shivered. Beside me, Rebecca put her hands over her mouth. I saw Luke take Maggie's hand and hold it. I wanted to hug them both.

Daniel's face was white and pinched, but he stood there in front of all the people he'd known for all of his life and he spoke to them. "Brothers and sisters, you will know that my mother and my baby sister recently nearly died. Both of them nearly lost their lives."

"I do not see," said Old Baldy sharply, "that this has anything to do with your request. Get to the point."

Daniel half turned so he could look at his father and the congregation. He took a deep breath and said in a quiet, desperate voice, "I ask to be allowed to return to school. I ask to be given permission to study at university." A pause, then the final, flat request. "I ask the community to give me permission to become a doctor so that I may serve you all."

Good one, Daniel! I felt like clapping and cheering. How could they say no to that? Now he could stay on with them and still be what he wanted to be. Then I noticed the shock waves rippling through the room.

Old Baldy got to his feet. He leaned on the lectern in front of him and skewered Daniel with his beady old eyes. "Request denied." He didn't even pray about it. "You know the teaching of the Rule, but I will repeat it for the benefit of any other son or daughter who may be entertaining such iniquitous thoughts: we of the Children of the Faith do not seek education beyond what the state decrees we must offer our children. To study at a university is to invite evil into your life." His voice thundered out. "It is to embrace godlessness and to open one's mind to unseemly sights, beliefs, and teachings." He struck the lectern and glared out at the congregation, particularly at the row where we sat.

"Now," he snapped at Daniel, "you will agree to accept the hand of Damaris Faithful in marriage. You will publicly admit your transgression and we will pray to the Lord to forgive your sins and cleanse you of all iniquitous thoughts." He rapped on the lectern with a knobbly knuckle. "We await your pledge."

Eternity passed before anyone in that hall breathed or spoke, but at last Daniel raised his head. I watched him, longing to get up and shout or throw my arms around him.

"I can make no pledge." Every ear strained to hear the whispered words. He raised his head and spoke directly to his father. "I can no longer stay in the Fellowship." Each word seemed to be forced out as if he didn't have enough air, or his throat was clamped tight. Something.

Uncle Caleb's face was gray with shock. Daniel dragged his eyes away and looked at Old Baldy. His voice was stronger as he said, "You are forcing me to break with my family. You are forcing me to leave. You forced Miriam to leave and now me." He dragged in a lungful of air. "I love them. I want to be with them, and you are making me leave. . . ."

His words were cut off by a babble of shouting. Then Damaris's father jumped up, yelling louder than all the rest. He waved his fists in the air and strode to the front of the stage, close to Daniel. "The work of the devil is with us this day! I call on you, my brothers and sisters, to strike at this evil before it contaminates us all!" His face was red and ugly. He drew back his arm and punched Daniel hard in the face. The other fist slammed into his ribs so that we heard the breath hiss out of him. He fell to the ground, and that great gorilla kept punching and kicking. Uncle Caleb didn't do anything. Nobody did anything. Stop him! Somebody was shouting the words—I think it was me—but no one made the smallest move to stop him hitting Daniel and kicking him.

I leapt up. "No!" I howled, and the children were crying and shouting beside me. I ran to the stage, grabbed Daniel's jacket and hauled him to the edge, kept pulling at him until he tumbled over, out of the way of those vicious fists and feet.

"Get up!" I tugged at him. "Get up! Let's get out of here!"

He stumbled to his feet, and I put my arm around him. His blood dripped onto my white blouse.

"Leave him, girl, on pain of damnation!" roared Old Baldy.

"Yes, leave me," Daniel whispered. "I will be all right." I said nothing, just hauled his arm over my shoulders to support him.

"You are both damned!" a voice thundered behind me. "Damned and cursed. Contaminators! You are both guilty of moral pollution!"

We had nearly reached where the children sat, clinging together in shock.

Old Baldy's voice boomed out behind us. "We expel you both from the Fellowship. Henceforth you are dead to us. Dead and gone."

Maggie wailed, a high, keening wail. Just as she had after we'd seen Miriam. I reached out and shook her hard. "Maggie! Listen, we're not dead! Look at me! Touch me! I'll just be somewhere else, not here. . . ."

There was a vicious shove in my back so that I tumbled forward to my knees, and now it was Daniel hauling at me to pick me up. "Good-bye," he whispered to the children. "Take care of each other."

Together we stumbled down the aisle that was longer than any marathon track in the world. I heard hissing and somebody actually spat onto the floor in front of us. Daniel was limping, and he leaned on me. I don't know if he was crying, but I was. Deep down inside myself where none of the hate-filled faces could see. But not for them, I wouldn't shed a tear for them. I caught sight of Damaris as we went. She pulled her skirt away as we passed her. My friend. She had been my friend.

Gideon balled his hands into fists and rocked on his toes.

We kept walking. There was nothing else we could do.

The door slammed shut behind us. We leaned against it for a moment. The sun was shining. That surprised me. I'd expected it to be dark outside, dark and with a full storm blowing.

"Let's get out of here!" I whispered. "I don't trust them a bit."

Daniel wiped at his face—tears and blood. "You are right, I think." He shook his head carefully, testing for loose bits. "We had better try to run."

"Why? You've still got the car keys!" I thought he would argue, but it seemed to settle him somehow.

"Of course. I forgot." Still leaning on me, he limped to the car.

I looked back as we left the car park, but the door to the Fellowship Center stayed shut. "Will they be all right?" I asked, more to myself than to him.

But he answered, savagely, "No, they will not be all right. Magdalene will grieve, Abraham and Luke will be treated more harshly in case they turn out like me, and the twins will have to do all their work and yours as well. My father will never be an Elder again."

I cried then, tears dribbling like a leaking tap. "Should I go back? Just till Mum comes back?"

"They would not accept you now. And if they did, just how long do you think you would last before you had another fit of hysterics at school?"

How did he know about that? "Bloody Beulah?" I asked.

He nodded.

"You're right. I know you're right. But Maggie . . ."

"Be quiet, Kirby," he said fiercely. "Do not make it worse than it is. Do you imagine I have not thought about all of this? Over and over again? Do you not think that I have tried to live by the Rule? Really tried, not like you. You always knew you could not live that way. It is not as difficult for you."

I gulped and swallowed my tears. He was right, but did he know just how bloody difficult it was? I glanced at him. The blood. The puffy eye. A rip in his jacket. Yeah. He knew.

We went to Mrs. Fletcher. She took us into her house, a house warm with books and music and with paintings on the walls. Photographs on the mantelpiece. Her husband and daughter returned the car to the Place of Fellowship, and she cleaned Daniel up. After she'd taken photos of the blood and bruises. "We may need evidence if you are to get a benefit to continue at school," she told him, her face grim.

I sat on her couch beside Daniel. Once again I was wearing everything I owned in the world. Again I was a refugee. *Mum, where are you, I need you.*

Mrs. Fletcher woke us in the morning. "Both of you are going to school today. It'll be better to keep your minds busy."

She'd organized another uniform for me. It was secondhand, but I didn't have to turn the waistband over. I brushed my hair with Mrs. Fletcher's hairbrush and cleaned my teeth with the new toothbrush she gave me, and as I did these things, I watched my reflection in the mirror.

"Kirby Greenland. Good morning, Kirby Greenland," I muttered at it. In the bedroom, I picked up Esther's clothes. I stood for a minute, holding them in my hands. What should I do with them? Throw them away? Put them through a shredder?

Suddenly, I decided to keep them. If ever I have children, I will show them the clothes. I will talk to them about what happened. I will not hide this part of their history.

I put the clothes on the bed. *I will, I will not.* I am Kirby, not Esther. Why, when I had fought not to change the way I spoke, was I doing it now?

I shivered. Esther wasn't going to vanish without a fight.

In the kitchen, Mrs. Fletcher waved at stuff set out on the bench. "Help yourself."

I grinned. Daniel would find all this casualness a bit different from home. He came in wearing jeans, a T-shirt, and a black eye. He held himself stiffly, as if his ribs hurt.

"The clothes fit well," Mrs. Fletcher said. He didn't have to wear a uniform because he was in his final year, but I guessed he'd have been a lot happier in one.

I waved a glass of orange juice at him. "Who's a cool dude, then?"

He smiled, he actually smiled. I jumped up and hugged him. "Sorry if that hurt, but I just wanted you to know you're a great guy, Daniel Pilgrim."

"You will never know, Kirby, how much you helped me. I thank you."

After breakfast, Mrs. Fletcher hustled us into her car. "Come on. I'm always late. Looks like today is no exception." It clearly didn't worry her.

I walked into my form room and sat waiting for Ms. Chandler to call the roll. Damaris and Charity weren't there. I wondered if they'd come. They were usually here by now. I watched the door, and words beat in my head. *Damned and cursed. We expel you both from the Fellowship. Henceforth you are dead to us. Dead and gone.*

Minutes later, the two girls walked in. I stared at them. I wanted to talk to them. I needed to talk to them. They must've worked out beforehand what they'd do, because they didn't hesitate, but walked to the other side of the room from where I sat.

I knew they'd do that. So why did it hurt so much?

Ms. Chandler called the roll. "Selina Amon."

"Yes."

"Hone Atutahi."

"Kia Ora."

"Avery Cardew."

"Yep."

"Charity Goodman."

"Present, Miss Chandler."

Damaris was the only other kid to answer "Present, Miss Chandler."

"Esther Pilgrim."

"Kirby. Call me Kirby Greenland. Please." I had

206

to clear my throat and blink my eyes hard. Damaris and Charity didn't look at me once.

Ms. Chandler asked me to stay after class. "Are you all right, Esther, sorry—Kirby?" She looked at me sharply.

I nodded. "I will be." I rubbed my forehead. "It's all a bit weird right now. It's kind of hard to adjust."

"Mrs. Fletcher told me what happened," she said briskly. "In my opinion, you are exceedingly lucky."

"I know," I mumbled, "it's just that . . ." My voice trailed off. How could she understand?

That day was so unreal. I kept swinging between Esther and Kirby. It was almost as if now that I didn't have to be Esther anymore, I wanted to be. It made me angry.

Daniel and I bought our lunch from the canteen with money Mrs. Fletcher had given us. It was the first time in his seventeen years he had ever bought food.

I told him about Damaris and Charity. He scrunched his paper bag into a ball and lobbed it into a bin. "What did you expect?"

"I know! But it hurts. We were friends." I tried to explain. "Friends are always there for each other."

"The Rule comes before friendship," Daniel said.

He stretched his arms out. "You have no idea how free I feel! I thought I would be frightened without the Rule, but it is wonderful." He turned to me. "Do you understand, Kirby?"

I nodded. Oh yes, I understood all right. What I didn't understand was why I kept feeling I should be speaking like Esther and dressing like Esther and, God help me, thinking like Esther. Thoughts skidded across the surface of my mind that appalled me. *They are right. You are evil. The Rule is good.*

I swallowed down the panic and tried not to think about it.

The man came back just before school finished. The man who'd come to the house asking for Kirby Greenland.

9

RORY ASHTON HAD COARSE BROWN hair cut ruthlessly short to stop it springing out from his head. He had big dark eyes, and he was solidly built.

He was my brother.

"Born when your mother was sixteen," explained Mrs. Fletcher as I sat in her office, stunned. "He wrote to your mother. Just before Christmas."

I stared at him. My brother? I was the second child my mother had abandoned? Then things started falling into place. I could almost hear them clanging. He must've written the letter that made her run away.

He was speaking to me. "I'm sorry," I said. "It's hard to concentrate."

I got a sharp look, as if he was thinking, *You're a few planks short of a bridge.*

"He wants to know," said Mrs. Fletcher patiently, "about your mother—his mother."

"Anything you can tell me," he said.

Of course he'd want to know. I just didn't feel up to telling him. Where could I start? The bell went as I was dithering around and making a right idiot of myself, then Daniel came in. "Daniel," said Mrs. Fletcher. "Meet your cousin."

The man—what was his name? He had a name, he'd told me what it was, and it had slid right out of my head the moment he'd said it. Anyway, he stared from Daniel, with his bruised face, back to me, and I was probably looking like an escapee from a straitjacket.

"Take them to get burgers for dinner, then deliver them back to my house," Mrs. Fletcher ordered. She held out some money.

The man shook his head. "I'll pay. It's no problem."

Daniel turned to Mrs. Fletcher. "Before we go, can you tell us what will be happening to us?"

She gave him a quick smile. "I've phoned your

uncle—where Miriam is staying. He says you're both to go to him. If you want to." She looked at me. "Kirby, you may prefer to go to your friend Louisa. There'll be no problem with a benefit now."

I couldn't think about that yet. I walked with the man—Rory, his name was Rory Ashton. I walked to his car. My cousin who felt like my brother was on one side of me and my brother who was a total stranger was on the other.

"Would you mind driving to the hospital first?" Daniel asked him.

"Sure, no problem," he said. If he was busting to know why, what with Daniel's spectacular bruises and all, he didn't ask. He didn't chatter either and I was grateful. If I'd been him, I'd be pestering me with questions, but he drove, Daniel gave directions, and other than that, we didn't talk.

"Would you like to come in?" Daniel asked him when we got there. "I am going to say good-bye to my baby sister. She is your cousin."

"Aunt Naomi, too?" I whispered.

Daniel's mouth twisted but he said calmly enough, "She would not see me. I will not make it difficult for her."

Rory Ashton snapped a look from one to the

other of us, but he still didn't nag me with questions. I liked that. I hauled myself out of the car, feeling a hundred years old. "It's the religion," I said, rubbing my head and holding onto the door. "It's breaking us all up. Tearing us apart." I gestured at Daniel. "They did that yesterday, then they threw us out. Now he can't see any of his family ever again. And my mother, my mother . . . I think when she was sixteen, I think . . ." I got all choked up. Again. It was becoming a habit.

Rory put a hand on my arm. "It's all right, Kirby. There's plenty of time. Take it easy." A sudden smile that warmed both Daniel and me. "At least I've found you. That was the hard part, believe me."

So we walked into the hospital together, the three of us. We went to the nursery and looked at Zillah. I couldn't say anything, and my eyes were hot, and I blinked to keep the tears from clogging my vision. Then we left.

Rory took us back to his motel. All he knew about his birth mother was that she was sixteen when he was born. He'd had a good childhood, he said. A good and happy life. "But now that I'm going to get married myself, I want to find out about her."

"What's so important about finding her just

because you're getting hitched?" I demanded. "If you'd left things alone, none of this would've happened."

"And my mother and Zillah would be dead," Daniel said softly. "It would have been much harder for me, too. Perhaps too hard."

What did he mean by that? I glared at him. "Okay! So I'm God's original little miracle, but I still wish—" I chucked a cushion at a wall. "Oh for God's sake, I don't know what I wish!" Or what I knew. Except that I was back in a motel, throwing things, and my life was upside down.

"When you get married," Rory said calmly, "it's a good idea to know your family history. See if there is a history of illness. That sort of stuff."

"Like extreme allergic reactions to letters out of the blue," I drawled.

"Do not be so antagonistic, Kirby!" Daniel said sharply. "You have the chance to learn the truth. Take it."

"Sorry," I muttered.

Rory patted my hand. "It's okay. I don't mind if you yell at me. I guess things have been pretty rough for both of you."

And that made me cry. Bloody hell!

Rory went and got the box of tissues from the bathroom, and while I tried to stop bawling, he told us how he'd written to Mum, and when there hadn't been any reply, he'd flown up from Christchurch and gone to our flat. The new people had sent him next door to Louisa. She had my letter, so she gave him the address, so here we all were.

I mopped some more at my face. "At least I know now why she ran away, I guess. But why didn't she just tell me? I wouldn't have minded." I looked at Rory. "I don't mind."

"You do not understand, Kirby," Daniel said quietly. "Think about Damaris and Charity. How would they feel if they had a child before they were married? I believe your mother must have felt deeply ashamed." He looked at Rory and smiled slightly. "I am sorry Rory, but you need to know how it is in our"—he stopped, then went on in the same quiet voice—"their, faith."

"I'm glad I escaped." Rory looked thoughtfully at the pair of us.

So I told him all about Mum, and it made me cry again, because I hadn't been able to really talk about her since she'd disappeared.

We went back to Mrs. Fletcher's via the

McDonald's drive-through. That made me laugh. For a start, it was the first time Daniel had ever been near a McDonald's. Rory raised his eyebrows, but only said, "So what do you want?" as he pulled up at the speaker.

I rattled off my favorite meal. Daniel looked around, puzzled. "Why are you asking? Should we not park the car and go inside?"

"No," I said. "This is magic. You talk to that box and it runs off and gets your food."

"May I take your order, please."

Daniel jumped. Rory gave his order and mine, and he looked at Daniel. "What'll you have, mate?"

Poor Daniel, he was still shell-shocked from the speaker, and how would he know what he wanted? "Give him the same as I'm having," I said.

We collected the orders and took them down to the lake to eat them.

Memories. Maggie wailing. Miriam reaching out her arms . . . Concentrate on here and now. On hamburgers and fries.

"Well, what do you think?" I asked Daniel through a mouthful of Big Mac.

"It is different," he said, polite as ever. "I do not think I would like it every day."

Back at Mrs. Fletcher's, she asked me where I wanted to stay until we found Mum. Part of me wanted to go back to Auckland and stay with Louisa. But only a part. I just couldn't imagine trying to explain everything to Gemma. I couldn't bear the thought of her saying how dumb it all was and weren't the kids wimps to stick with it. She'd never understand. Just as I wouldn't have.

"I'd like to go with Daniel."

"I am glad," he said, and smiled at me. Yes, it would be good to be with Daniel a while longer. We could help each other into the world.

"But what about Mum?" I asked. "I have to find her, Mrs. Fletcher. I have to find out what's happened to her."

She flicked my hair. "I know, duckie. I'll . . ."

"I'll still be looking," Rory broke in. "I'll keep in touch. Tell you everything I find out." He gave me a crooked grin. "I really want to meet her now. Before, all I wanted was the medical stuff. But now—well, she's more like a real person."

I smiled at him, suddenly pleased he was there.

After he'd gone, Mrs. Fletcher looked thoughtfully at my uniform. "You can hardly turn up in Wellington wearing that and with nothing else to your name," she said. "Where are your own clothes?"

"At my father's house," Daniel said. "In the garage along with her mother's clothes."

"I'll phone him at work tomorrow and arrange to collect everything," she said. "What about your gear, Daniel?"

"He doesn't want it," I broke in. "It's the pits."

So the next day we went to school until it was time to catch the bus to Wellington. I wanted to go and say good-bye to Maggie.

"You cannot," Daniel said flatly. "Do not upset her further. It might help you, but it will not help her."

"But I only want to—"

"She has to live by the Rule. You do not. Do not split her loyalties, Kirby. It is not fair."

Nothing was fair. I kept my mouth shut until I could be sure I wouldn't bawl.

We collected my clothes on the way to the bus station with Mrs. Fletcher. The bags—mine and Mum's—were stacked at the gate. If my uncle had written all over them KEEP OUT: CONTAMINATOR, the message couldn't have got much clearer.

I don't care. I don't. So why does my throat ache?

"I asked your uncle if he knew your mother hadn't gone to Africa," she said when Daniel and I got back in the car.

"What did he say?"

"He said, 'I have airmail letters from my sister. She says she is in Africa. I believe her.'"

She mimicked my uncle's gray voice to perfection, but I couldn't smile. "So she didn't tell him, either."

She took a hand off the wheel and patted my arm. "Try not to worry, Kirby. Rory's working on it, and Jim—your uncle—is on it as well."

Try not to worry! How?

At the bus depot, I rummaged in my bags until I found some shorts and a shirt that I tied at the waist. Kirby. This was definitely Kirby. Daniel blinked a bit, but he smiled when he saw me. I handed the uniform back to Mrs. Fletcher and hugged her. "Thank you!" I wanted to say more, but I got all choked up. She laughed and pushed me in the direction of the bus.

The bus pulled out. We said nothing. Daniel's face was calm. I wondered what he was thinking, but I didn't ask him. Later, we talked about Mum and about Rory. "Were you shocked?" I asked. "About Mum having a baby before she was married, I mean."

He smiled, a sort of twisted smile. "To be honest, Kirby, I was. I know these things happen outside, but I have never heard of it happening to any of our women."

"You don't want to be shocked, do you?"

"No," he sighed, "I do not. I want to understand." He rubbed at a bruise on his face. "Was she tempted, or did a man wrong her?"

"Oh, Daniel! You'll have to learn to talk differently if you're going to be a doctor!"

He was surprised. "Why? What words would you use?"

"I have been wondering," I said slowly, "if she had sex with a man to get back at her parents, or if . . ." I couldn't say it.

"If what?"

Didn't he know? Couldn't he guess?

"Or if she was raped," I whispered.

Miriam and the uncle whose name was Jim met us. Miriam was lit up as if she'd swallowed her own private source of light. She threw her arms around Daniel. "It's so good to have you here! It's so good!" Some of the stiffness drained out of Daniel's shoulders. "You look well, little sister." I wondered if it was a strain for him not to comment on her clothes. She was wearing jeans and a cutoff top that showed a good two inches of skin.

"Well, that's more than I can say for you!" The smile left her face and she leaned over and touched the bruises around his eye. "What did they do to you, Daniel?"

Jim interrupted. "Leave it till we get home, Miriam. Then he won't have to go over it twice."

They were great to us, the whole family—Jim, my auntie Nina, and the three kids who'd all left home, but popped in to welcome us. Harry was the oldest and was into computers and waterskiing; next was Miranda—twenty-one and leaving next week for Los Angeles. Jeff was the baby. "He's twenty," said his mother, "and thank heavens he's found his own flat now."

Nina—she said to drop the aunt bit, it made her feel ancient—had a huge afternoon tea laid out to welcome us. We sat around the table and talked until the sun went down.

"Thank Christ you had the sense to get out when you did, Dad," said Harry, shuddering.

Jim glanced at Daniel. "Go easy on the language for a day or two, Harry."

"Thank you," Daniel said, "but it does not worry me."

"And before long," Miriam grinned, "we'll have you saying *doesn't* instead of *does not*."

"You have found it easy to change?" he asked her.

She grabbed his hand and held on to it hard. "No, Daniel, don't think that." She jumped to her feet. "Wait. I'll show you." She ran from the room and returned moments later clutching a large brown folder. "Here. Look at these." She opened the folder. It was full of paintings and drawings. She jabbed at the top one. "My counselor made me start painting again. This was the first one. Look at it!"

We stared at it. I swallowed and blinked hard to clear my vision. It was shocking. She'd painted flowers, trees, birds, and fragments of Bible quotes, and they were all in murky colors and all twisted and wrenched out of shape. There was the silhouette of a person with holes for eyes. The painting shrieked of suffocation, of being pushed into an unnatural shape, of pain.

She flicked through those first paintings as if she couldn't bear to look at them. "Look. I did this when I knew you were coming."

Bright colors surrounded a girl sitting in the middle

of the painting. It was Miriam. Two shadowy figures emerged from mistiness at the bottom left, and these were balanced at the top right by another hollow-eyed figure struggling to see through black fog. Maggie.

I couldn't look at it. So much pain. I flicked the pages. They were all there—the twins, Maggie, Daniel, Abraham at his boldest, Luke with his shy glance, and Aunt Naomi and Uncle Caleb.

"You couldn't have stopped, could you?" I asked.

She shook her head. "I tried. I really did. But my hands seem to have other ideas. And then somehow Ira heard that one of my paintings was displayed in the library and that was the end." She touched Daniel's hand. "It still isn't easy. I still cry a lot, but mostly I've stopped wondering if I was right to run away." She smiled at Jim and Nina. "You two are so patient with me, I don't know how you do it."

Jim chuckled, and glanced at his own three kids. "We've had plenty of practice."

"Thanks a bunch, Dad." Miranda laughed. She turned to me, her face bright. "Were you stunned to find you had a brother, Kirby?"

Mrs. Fletcher had told them about Mum and Rory. I nodded. "But it makes sense. I can kind of understand why she took off now." I looked at Jim. "Did you know about the baby? About Rory. Before Mrs. Fletcher told you, I mean?"

He shook his head and his face was grim. "No." He sighed. "I'd better tell you about the day they threw her out." His fingers were shredding a bread roll. Nina quietly put her hand over his.

He shook his shoulders. His voice was flat and unemotional as he told the story of my mother's eviction from her home. "It was her sixteenth birthday. A Wednesday, and she was supposed to be getting married the following Saturday. That morning my younger brother Isaac came bursting in when I was having breakfast shouting to Mother that Martha was very sick and she was lying on the bathroom floor."

He stopped. Isaac. I didn't remember anybody called Isaac. Where was he now?

"Well?" Harry said. "What happened next?"

Jim pulled his mouth down in a grimace. "I went off to work. Illness was women's stuff, and of course, being unmarried, I'd never heard about morning sickness. Such things were never discussed where a young man might hear them." He leaned his arms on the table and looked directly at me.

"Kirby, when I got home from work that night my sister had gone. At family prayers that night my father said he had cast her out because she was full of sin. "I will not have her under my roof," he thundered. "She will contaminate you all."

Now, where had I heard that before?

"Didn't you ask what she'd done?" Jeff asked.

"You don't ask. . . ." Miriam and I said automatically.

"And if you do, you do not get told," Daniel added.

Jim nodded. "That's right. But I did ask and I said, 'But she was sick this morning. How could you cast her out?'" He rubbed his temples. "He told us nothing, just prayed and ranted and prayed some more. Mother had been crying, and a couple of Elders came round and there was more ranting. But that night when I was getting ready for bed, I dropped my toothbrush, and when I bent down to get it, I saw blood splashed on the wall."

"He'd beaten her up?" I felt sick in my stomach.

"Yes, he'd beaten her up. I went crazy. Went for him, and we had an out-and-out fistfight, and all the kids were screaming and crying." He took a breath. "But the old bastard wouldn't tell me anything. In the end, I told him to rub me out of the book too, because I was going after Martha, and I left."

"Did you try to find Mum?" I asked, my voice wobbling a bit.

He sighed. "Yes, I found her. It took me three days, but I found her. She was in hospital because my dear father had broken her jaw." I closed my eyes, and my stomach heaved. "She wouldn't tell me why she'd been thrown out. I wanted us to stick together, but she said she already had a job. She was going to live on a farm out the back of Gisborne and be the housekeeper." He stared out the lounge windows to where the lights were blinking on in the city below us. "She said she'd write, but she never did. We completely lost touch—and now I know why."

"She's good at disappearing," I whispered.

"We'll find her this time," Miriam cried. "Won't we, Jim?"

Instead of reassuring me, Jim pushed his cup away and cleared his throat.

"Jim?" I croaked. "What is it? You know something?"

Nina got up and put her arms around me. "Kirby, darling, we know where she is." She held tightly to my shoulders. "She's ill, Kirby. She's here in

Wellington, in hospital, and she's very ill."

I pushed her away and jumped up. "Why didn't you tell me? I should be there! I should be with her!"

Pictures of my mother lying still in a hospital bed raced through my head.

Nina pressed down on my shoulders, making me sit down again. "It's not that sort of ill, Kirby. She's had a breakdown. She's in a psychiatric ward."

10

MRS. FLETCHER HAD TOLD THEM it was possible that my mother had had a breakdown, they said, so they'd asked around the hospitals.

"She's crazy," I whispered. "My mother's crazy."

"She's not," Jim said briskly. "But she is depressed."

Depressed? I didn't understand. "Louisa used to get depressed, but she'd clean all the windows, dig the garden, and spend an hour talking with Mum and she'd be okay again." Depressed couldn't mean she was very ill. Not ill enough to run away and dump me.

"Listen, Kirby," Nina said, sitting down beside me. "Your mother was found at the airport. She'd been sitting there for around twenty-four hours, just staring into space. She couldn't tell anyone who she was or where she lived. They took her to hospital and she's been on medication. . . ."

"You mean drugs?" I asked in a high, thin voice that didn't sound like mine. I had this awful picture of my mother sitting in the airport, staring at ghosts.

Nina grabbed my hand and somebody, Miriam, I think, put an arm around my shoulders. "She's a lot better now, but . . ." She hesitated.

"But what?" I was cold and shivering. The arm tightened around my shoulders.

"She seems better, she's started looking after herself again." What did that mean? Nina saw the shock in my face and said gently, "When people are as depressed as she was they haven't got the energy to get out of bed, have a shower, care about how they look. Each morning, they've had to persuade her to do all that, Kirby."

I heard a howl, like a wounded animal, and I noticed Daniel looking at me, his eyes full of pain.

Nina shook my hands, squeezing them hard. "Listen Kirby. She's come out of that stage now.

She's talking and she's much better, but they're worried because they feel some of the improvement is just an act. They think she's doing it out of willpower rather than because she's better."

I knew all about that willpower. I stood up. "I want to see her. She needs me. I've always looked after her. I have to see her."

Jim got up. "I'll take you, Kirby. But—she may not want to see you. You have to be prepared."

I stared at them. She may not want to see me? Miriam looked down, and Daniel's face might as well have been carved out of white marble. They knew all about parents not wanting to see their kids.

Jim drove me to the hospital. We didn't talk—I don't think I could have. He was leading me through corridors when I managed to whisper, "Have you seen her? Would she see you?"

He took my arm and held it. "No, Kirby, she didn't want to see me. But she does know you were coming to live with us."

I could not begin to imagine how it would be if my mother refused to see me.

"This is it," Jim said. I stood in a wide corridor while he went up to the office. I looked around. There was a big room I could see into. People sat staring at a television. There was canned laughter, but nobody smiled, they just stared. Then a weird woman raced out of the room, babbling hysterically.

Jim took my arm again. "We'll wait in here." He nodded at the woman he'd spoken to in the office. "Sue will go and tell her you're here."

I slid my hand down so I could grab hold of his. In the doorway of the big room we collided with the weird woman. She had a suitcase now, with clothes falling out of it. "Gotta go. Things to see, people to do. Gonna stand for parliament. Do the garden . . ."

A couple of people came up to her and took her arms. "Come along, Katie," the man said. "We'll just have a talk about this first."

"Time for some more medicine, too, don't you think?" The woman smiled at her. But they held her firmly and steered her off down the corridor.

I was shaking. Had Mum been like that? I looked around at the blank faces in the room we were entering. I'd rather she'd been like that than like these people who sat and stared and saw nothing. Jim let go my hand and put his arm around my shoulders instead.

She came. I looked up, and she was there in the doorway, staring at me. "Mum!" I shrieked and I hurtled across the room and into her arms. "Mum! Oh, Mum!" It was all I could say, and I was laughing and tears were pouring down my face. She was crying too, crying and saying, "Forgive me, Kirby, I'm so sorry, I'm so sorry!"

We stood there, hugging each other for ages, then I led her gently to a chair and sat her down. She was so thin, I was scared she'd break. I collapsed onto the floor at her feet, leaned on her knee, and held her hand. "Oh, Mum, you didn't have to run away! Why didn't you tell me? Why didn't you tell me the Elders were on to you? We could've got the police to stop them—anything!"

She stroked my hair and said through more tears, "I know, Kirby. I know that now. The guilt! I've had to deal with all that guilt. Abandoning you!" She shivered as the tears kept coming. "Do you hate me?"

I looked up at her, a ghost of the mother I knew. "Of course I don't hate you!" I said. *Not now, anyway. But I did, Mum, I hated you so much.* "And when you get out of here we'll get a flat and I'll look after you and we'll be happy again." I shut out the fleeting thought that I didn't know how to look after my mother anymore. I would have to do it, there was no one else.

I looked around for Jim, but he'd disappeared into the passage. Quickly, I asked her something that had been puzzling me. "Mum, how come you raced off so quickly to go to Africa? I mean, something like that can't be organized in two seconds. Can it?"

She shook her head. "When Caleb and the Elders started coming, I wrote away about it. I figured it would help if I knew I had an escape—I never really meant to go. I never intended to leave you."

"But the letters—you wrote and said you were in Africa."

More tears slid down her face. "I couldn't tell you I was here. I just couldn't."

Another thought occurred to me. "How did you manage to leave the hospital so quickly? You didn't have extra holidays, did you?"

She shook her head again. "No." Her hands twisted against themselves as she whispered, "I told them my mother was ill. I said she'd had a stroke and I had to go and care for her."

Sue—I discovered later that she was a nurse—came in. "How's it going?" Her eyes swept over Mum, missing nothing.

"This is my daughter, Kirby," Mum said, wiping

her eyes. Every little thing seemed to make her cry, and she looked so tired.

I stood up. "Mum, I'll come and see you again tomorrow."

She pushed herself out of the chair and put her arms around me. "That will be lovely, darling."

I bit my lip. I knew her, and I knew she was saying what she thought she ought to be saying. Oh, Mum.

I was halfway across the room when I remembered Rory. "Mum"—I turned back and took her hands again—"by the way, I know about Rory. I've met him. He's nice. You'll be proud of him."

"Rory?" She was puzzled. Sue stood beside her, still.

"Yes," I said. "You know. He wrote to you before Christmas." She just kept staring at me. I shook her hands. "Mum! The baby you had when you were sixteen! He wrote to you! And you ran away." I gulped and swallowed. I noticed Sue's face. She looked as if she'd been given the key to a puzzle. But Mum had gone blank, and she looked just like the other people around the room. She was staring at nothing again. "Mum!" I shrieked, but she didn't respond. She just stood there completely blank.

"Stay here, Kirby," Sue said, "I'll see to Ellen, then I'll come and talk to you."

Jim came back, sat me down in a chair, and held my hand. What had I done? When Sue returned she said, "That's good. She can really begin the healing process now."

"But she looked . . ." I shuddered and glanced around me.

"I know." Sue's voice was very calm and comforting. "She's had a relapse. But it's out in the open now. We thought there was something she couldn't talk about. That was too painful. She'll be bad for two or three days, but then she'll start to get better. Really better, this time."

"How long?" I managed to ask.

"Don't try to see her for at least a week," Sue said. "And she won't be ready to leave here for maybe a month. It depends a bit on how she responds to the drugs now that she is finally dealing with this."

Jim took me home, and I cried all the way.

Life settled into a pattern. We went to school, came home, I'd phone the hospital to see how Mum was, and we'd do our homework. Nina worked, so the three of us kids cooked dinner.

After ten days, Mum asked to see me. She looked awful, and everything I said made her cry. It's normal, they said. She's getting better. She's talking about the baby, about what had happened. She got a bit worse again for a day or two after she finally told how she'd got pregnant. An Elder had asked her father to let Mum work for him, and then he'd ordered her to submit to him. It went on for two months, and she'd been too terrified to tell anyone.

Rory phoned every few days to see how she was. "God, the poor woman," he said, when he heard. I wondered how he felt about his father, but I couldn't bring myself to talk to him about it.

Once Mum started getting better and I could see the improvement, I stopped worrying so much about her. But I had time to think about myself. I realized I was loving living in a real family. The realization that came two seconds after that was not so hot: I did not want to go back to just Mum and me. She was getting better, she'd be out soon. It was what I'd wanted for weeks. I shrugged. No good thinking about what'd happen then.

Instead, I got busy. I joined a gym and made

Miriam join, too. I went five times a week, but she'd only come twice.

"Get a life," she said, if I nagged her to come more.

"I've got a life."

"I noticed," she said, stretching out on the bed and pushing her sketching pad out of the way. "Gym every day, then you drag Daniel off to acting class. . . ."

"He's so good!" I broke in. "You should see him. He's a riot!"

She ignored me. "And now you've taken on the brat next door. . . ."

"She's only a brat because she can't read and she feels bad because Danielle can and she's two years younger than Marguerite so Marguerite does the brat act so's people will growl at her and not notice she's dumb." I ran out of breath. "So that's why I'm teaching her to read."

Miriam rolled over on her stomach. "It's great. And her mother's over the moon. I just think you should slow down a bit. I mean, you go and see your mother every day on top of all that."

"I can do it. I like being busy." And wasn't that just the truth? Be so busy that my life was filled up every single second, so I'd have things to remember when it was just Mum and me. At least that was my story, even to myself.

I could see the improvement in Mum each time I visited. After a month, she looked better. Her hair was shiny again, and she wore lipstick. "I went for a drive in the van today," she said. "We went up to see the windmill. It's so high up there, I thought I was a bird."

I went to the gym nine times that week. Miriam yelled at me, and even Daniel said, "Don't you think you're doing a little too much, Kirby?"

It was all right for him. Nina had made him go to the same counselor Miriam had gone to, and every day he looked more relaxed and happy. She tried to make me go too, but I didn't need it. I was fine as long as I was busy.

After another week, Mum said she wanted to meet Rory. He came to visit afterward. "That bloody goddamned religion's got a lot to answer for," he said savagely. He looked at me. "I'll come again, Kirby, when she's stronger. I'll bring Jenny—my fiancée. We'll keep in touch."

Eight days later they said she could leave the hospital the following week.

I cooked complicated meals every night after that.

I doubled the time I spent with Marguerite. I stayed at the gym until it closed. When I got home on Friday night, Daniel gave me a message from Mum: "The psychologist needs to talk to us both before I leave. I've made an appointment for 11 A.M. Monday."

I stared at the piece of pink paper, where Daniel's writing was wobbling around in a most odd way. The end. This was the end.

I threw myself into the weekend. The whole family was exhausted by Sunday night.

"My feet are so sore!" Nina groaned, and lay down on the floor, propping her legs up on the sofa.

"You're nuts," Miriam said. "Next time you get the urge to climb Mount Kaukau, you can do it by yourself."

I didn't go to school on Monday morning, couldn't stand the thought of sitting still until it was time to go to the hospital. Instead, I went to the gym.

I sat on the bus that took me to the hospital and considered the meeting ahead. The psychologist would tell me how to look after Mum and give me all sorts of instructions I didn't need. *For chrissakes, I know how to look after my goddamned mother, I've only been doing it all my goddamned life.*

I clapped my hands over my mouth. Had I said that out loud? Nobody was staring at me, so perhaps I hadn't.

I got off the bus a stop too soon so that I had to run the rest of the way. It felt good to be moving.

Sue met me at the office. "Hello, Kirby. I'll take you through to Allan's office." She smiled over her shoulder. "He's the psychologist Ellen's been working with."

I grunted. Great. But I didn't want to work with him. He couldn't tell me anything.

They were both in there. Mum got up and hugged me. She held my shoulders and looked at me hard for a few seconds, then she sighed and muttered, "'The sins of the fathers . . .'"

"I know that quote," I said brightly.

"Sit down, Kirby." Allan waved at a chair that reminded me of the ones in Mrs. Fletcher's office.

I sat. "I don't know why you wanted me to come today," I babbled. "I know how to look after my mother. There's nothing you can tell me." I jumped up. "Come on, Mum. Let's go. We have to find a flat. We'd better get on with it."

My mother didn't move except to rub her hand across her eyes. "Oh, Kirby!"

"This appointment is for an hour," Allan said. "So why don't you sit down?"

I glared at Mum. "We don't need this, Mum! It's just a waste of time!"

She looked at me then, her eyes full of tears. Again. Was she ever going to stop crying? "Do you remember the day I left?" she asked huskily.

As if I could ever forget. "Yeah."

"I don't remember much of it," she said, speaking as if her voice hurt her. "But I do remember saying I didn't want you to end up like me. Running and running because you were too frightened to stand still." She reached for my hand, but I snatched it away. "What is it, Kirby? What are you running from?"

I backed into a corner and glared at the pair of them. "Nothing!"

"Ellen spoke of the sins of the fathers," Allan observed as if he was discussing the weather. "Children learn patterns of behavior from their parents. Ellen is watching you deal with your current problems by keeping so busy you can't think. Just the way she coped with hers. Before her breakdown."

I could run for it. They couldn't lock me in.

"I have discovered you can't run forever, Kirby." My mother's voice was stronger now. "You have to tell me what is worrying you."

"You're a great one to say that!" I scoffed. "You wouldn't talk to me. You didn't even tell me about Africa or Rory or . . . anything!" I pushed my hands hard against the wall behind me. "Don't talk to me about talking." I gasped for air, and the terrible words I didn't want to say tumbled out of my mouth. "I hate you!" I slid down the wall sobbing wildly, my hands over my face. "I shouldn't have come. I didn't want to come. I don't . . . it isn't . . . I didn't mean . . ."

A hand on my shoulder. "Kirby. It's all right." Mum. And she wasn't crying. She even sounded sort of calm and strong. "You're allowed to hate me. Believe me, I've hated myself for more years than you've been alive." I couldn't look at her. *This is my mother who I've loved forever, and now I've just told her I hate her.*

"But I don't," I whispered. "I love you. I want you to get out of here and I want us to live together again. . . ." I couldn't say any more, because it wasn't true. I did love her, but I hated her, too. And I didn't want to live with her, but if I didn't I'd feel so guilty and be so miserable about it that I might as well go and live with her in the first place.

She was talking. Saying something. "What did you say?" The words didn't make sense.

"I said I don't think we'll live together again. Not for a while, anyway."

Sheer rage burned through me. "So you're dumping me again!"

"Stop." That was Allan. "You are allowed to be angry, Kirby. But be angry at the right things. Right now, I'd say you're using anger to cover up a feeling of guilt."

I turned on him, snarling. "What would you know about it? Since when did you get inside my head? Keep your smart remarks for my mother. She seems to love them."

"Kirby," snapped my mother, "I will not have you behaving like this! Sit down, shut up and do some thinking." She pointed at the chair I'd sat in.

I stayed where I was. Let them do the I-know-better-than-you act. Let them think they could psychoanalyze me into a corner. What did I care?

"Are you enjoying being in a corner with your back against the wall?" Allan asked.

I glared at him.

"Answer the question," Mum said.

I stared at her, but she didn't look away, and her

chin was set with just as much determination as mine. I tried again to keep my mouth shut, but the words kept coming from somewhere inside me. "All right!" I burst out. "You want it, you can have it! But just remember—you asked for it!" I was panting, and there was sweat pouring down my back, and stinging my eyes. My hands were pressed flat against the wall again. "I don't want to live with you! I need somebody to look after me. Me!" I unglued a hand from the wall and thumped my chest. "Thanks to what you did to me I don't know who I am any longer. I have dreams at night and I'm Esther again and I'm happy because I'm living the Rule." I rubbed my face, it seemed to be wet. "D'you know what that feels like? Do you? It feels like there's a rope stuck around each of your ankles and they're being pulled in different directions. And, if I don't have that dream, I dream I'm in a dark corner and there are people in black clothes and they're damning me and cursing me to Hell." I sobbed for breath and my chest hurt. "That's why I do things. That's why I can't stop. I have to be tired. I have to be tired so I'll sleep."

Silence. Mum wasn't crying. She sat very still, but she wasn't crying, and she kept her eyes steady on mine. I looked away and worked at getting some air in my lungs.

"What do you think about in the daytime if you let yourself stop?" Allan asked.

What the hell. It couldn't get much worse than it already was. I slid down so I sat on the floor and let my head fall onto my knees. "I think about having a mother. A real mother. Like Nina."

The silence pounded around the room in time to the pulse in my head. I couldn't look at my mother. I loved her so much and I hated her so much and now I'd probably killed her. How was I going to live with it? I'd be running so fast I'd burn out in a month. Or a day.

"I want to know," I managed to say at last, "I want to know how you can love somebody but hate them as well."

My mother came and put her arms around me. "It is a miracle to me, Kirby, that you can still love me at all." She stroked my head. "We have a long way to go, you and I. But I think the running can stop now. For both of us."

I was so tired. It was all I could do to nod. My mind was stunned. I'd said all those awful things. The things I'd been so busy trying to keep out of my head, and they hadn't killed her. She was the one comforting me. I couldn't believe it. "You're being a mother," I muttered.

She gave a sort of choke. "Don't you think it's about time, my darling?"

We sat there forever, Mum with her arms around me and me just leaning against her. After a long time, I lifted my head. "But I can't let you live somewhere else. I just can't do it."

"It's not your decision," said my mother, who'd never made a big decision as long as I'd been able to remember, "it's mine." The love in her eyes soothed the sore places inside me. "I think I'll need about three months to get really well again. We can make some decisions then."

So she went to stay with a woman who'd once been sick the way Mum had. We phoned each other every day. Often, she met us after school and came home on the train with us. While we cooked tea, she'd do some ironing or just sit and chat to us. At first she was a bit reserved around Jim, until he started teasing her like he did us kids. One evening when we were having a barbecue with the whole family, including Rory and Jenny, she said, "I never knew how great it could be to have relatives."

Sometimes we went for walks, just the two of us, and she told me what it was like for her as a kid.

"I wouldn't have understood before," I murmured. "I'd never have known why you just didn't . . ." I spread my hands, unable to say more.

She pulled her mouth down in a funny smile. "There's nothing like walking in somebody else's shoes to understand what makes them tick."

In June, she got a part-time job and moved into a flat. "Can I come and stay for the weekend?" I asked. Part of me wanted to and part of me didn't. But I went and we laughed a lot, but what was different was that she cooked and did the washing and looked after herself and me. She also told me to go to bed and tape the rest of the movie to watch the next day. "Hey, you're taking this mother stuff a bit seriously!" I grumbled, but I went off to bed grinning like a clown. It seemed I had a mother, I really did.

On Sunday night, she sat me down at the table. "By Christmas, Kirby, I should be working full-time again. And I want you to come back home." She looked steadily at me. "You belong with me and I want you."

I nodded. "Yes," I said. "I do. I'll come." It was

that easy. I knew I'd miss living with Miriam and Daniel, Nina and Jim. But I belonged with Mum. And she wanted me. She didn't need me. Not now. But she wanted me. Suddenly we were grinning at each other, and she flung her arms around me, and we didn't know if we were laughing or crying.

In July, there was a thing on one of those current affairs programs on telly about the Children of the Faith. I was scared, and part of me didn't want to watch it.

"Why not?" Miriam demanded, when I told her and Daniel as we caught the train to school. "I can't wait."

"What if it turns me into Esther again? She's gone now. I haven't had the dreams for ages."

Daniel looked thoughtful. "Maybe it'll finally bury Esther forever. I'm looking forward to it. I hope they show the children. And Mother." I didn't blame him for not wanting to see Uncle Caleb.

"It won't make you howl your eyes out?" I asked.

"Probably. But I'll put up with that for the chance of seeing them again."

That night, Mum came over so we could all watch the program together. Jim set the video to record and we put the new tape in that we'd bought specially.

The reporter stood in front of the Place of Fellowship. "Twenty-three families who worship here," he gestured behind him, "are today packing up and moving to Nelson. The Children of the Faith believe that true salvation lies in following the teachings of the Bible literally. They live by what they call the Rule. They have no telephones, television, or radios. They do not read books or newspapers. They keep their thoughts turned to the Lord. Their women are modest, their men devout, and their children obedient." He walked toward the door, with the camera following him. "Their leader is Ezra Faithful."

Old Baldy's face jumped out at us. The camera zoomed out to show him in long shot, dressed in his dark suit and shiny shoes. He was on the stage of the Fellowship Center, with his arms raised and his eyes closed. There was a voice-over of the announcer explaining about the Rule and how they wanted to live apart from the iniquities of the world. "We are not permitted to speak to any of the members of the Fellowship," the reporter said, "but the Elders have kindly given permission for us to film the exodus, as they are calling it, to Nelson."

The next sequence was of Charity's family packing belongings into boxes. Charity was wrapping crockery in plain white paper. No newspaper allowed. Then the camera showed Thomasina and her baby. A boy with big ears, wearing a long gown. The camera lingered on Thomasina's face. She looked so young. Another shot of Talitha and her family singing after dinner, boxes stacked neatly around the walls behind them.

"They've got to show them!" Daniel muttered. Miriam was biting her lips.

But the next shot was of a convoy of laden cars and a sign that said WELLINGTON. Then we saw them driving onto the ferry. Old Baldy came out on deck and the Children of the Faith followed him.

"There's Luke!"

But it was only a fleeting glimpse. They all gathered around while Old Baldy prayed for a safe crossing. "Praise the Lord."

The camera shifted to a view of a gray sea with tossing, whitecapped waves. Then it came back to the ferry, and there they were. Aunt Naomi in her long skirt and head scarf stood looking back at the city. What was she thinking? What was behind that calm expression? Was she thinking about the children she'd lost—about Miriam and Daniel? Maybe even about me?

The children came to stand beside her. Rebecca carried Zillah all wrapped up in a beautiful shawl, and Rachel held Maggie's hand. Zillah cried, and Maggie touched her cheek, spoke to her, and the camera zoomed in for a close-up of Zillah laughing up at Maggie. Rachel and Rebecca smiled at both of them. Abraham and Luke's eyes were everywhere, but they stayed quiet, beside their mother.

We sighed as the shot faded.

The ferry moved out into the harbor as the camera zoomed in to show a close-up of the couple standing at the rail. It was Damaris and Gideon, together, but not touching. Her beautiful face filled the screen for several seconds. As I looked at her, all I felt was pity that her life would be so narrow, that she wasn't going to be able to think for herself, that she lived by a Rule which said *Thou shalt not* rather than *You can—give it a go, try it, and see what happens.*

The final shot was of the ferry sailing out to sea.

Esther wasn't there. Daniel was right. She was dead.